Contents

366 Days of Short Tales

91 INSPIRING CHILDREN'S BEDTIME STORIES

WITH BIG LESSONS

Winter Volume

Ella Casey Morgan

ISBN 978-9925-8148-6-2
Book Cover by Getcovers.com
Illustrations by Stella Connors
1st Edition 2024

Introduction

Once upon a time, in the classroom of a young teacher filled with curious minds and inquisitive eyes, stories began to bloom. These weren't just any stories, mind you. They were tales spun from the threads of everyday life, woven with the shyness of a new friend, the fierce possessiveness of a best friend, and the struggles of those who fight to believe in themselves.

As a teacher, I saw these moments unfold, and later, as a parent, I witnessed a whole new chapter begin. The joys and jealousies of siblings, the messy rooms and study sessions, the way friendships blossomed, and hobbies took flight – these everyday experiences became the muse that guided my pen.

But instead of lectures or scoldings, I dreamed of a gentler way to plant the seeds of kindness, empathy, and strength. What if bedtime stories could become magical lessons? Stories that would empower children to face the joys and challenges of our modern world, stories that would make them kinder, braver, and truer to themselves.

And so, this collection was born. 366 tales, one for each day of the year. Each story holds a tiny treasure, a value to be discovered, a lesson to be learned. Perhaps within these pages, your child will find the strength to overcome a fear, the courage to stand up for what is right, or the spark of empathy to light up another's life. If even one child feels more empowered, or better equipped to handle life's challenges after reading these stories, then this endeavor will have been worthwhile. It is my sincere wish that these tales will inspire and uplift, helping to cultivate the next generation of compassionate and confident individuals.

So, snuggle up close and let the adventure begin. Within these stories lies the potential for a little one to grow, dream, and become the best version of themselves!

Ella

A Crow and Three Geese

Coby the Crow perched on a high branch, feeling like a lump of black coal next to the sparkling pond below. Three geese, Gabby, Gus, and Greta were gliding across the water like elegant white boats. "Ugh," Coby grumbled, "why are they so white and fancy? Maybe if I took a long bath with them, I would turn white too!"

With a splash, Coby flopped into the pond. He copied the geese, dunking his head and flapping his wings like a flailing windmill. Water sprayed everywhere, soaking a very surprised frog who was sunbathing on a lily pad. "Hey there, scruffy!" the geese honked, surprised to see Coby splashing around. "I'm going to be white and beautiful just like you!" Coby cawed, feathers dripping.

Gabby and the other geese exchanged confused looks. They didn't want to hurt Coby's feelings, but... well, turning white wasn't exactly in the crow handbook. Coby kept splashing, turning the pond into a feathery soup. After what felt like forever (and probably scared away all the fish), the sun started to set, and all the pond inhabitants prepared for bedtime.

Exhausted, Coby finally climbed out, shivering uncontrollably like a chick. He peeked at his reflection in the water. Yikes! Still black as the dark night. "Aw, man," Coby drooped. "Why didn't I turn white?" Gus the Goose waddled over kindly. "Coby," he said, "we geese are born white. You crows, well, you get awesome black feathers. Like a superhero cape, but for birds!" Greta the Goose added, "Everyone's special in their own way. Colors don't matter. Look at me, I trip over my own webbed feet all the time!"

Everyone giggled, even the little turtle resting nearby. Coby felt a tiny bit better. Maybe being black wasn't so bad after all. "You know what?" Coby said, with a small smile. "You're right. Black feathers are pretty cool. Plus, I can swoop down really fast and scare the pigeons away. They hate that!" From that day on, Coby the Crow embraced his black brilliance, soaring through the sky with newfound confidence. After all, being unique was way more fun than trying to be someone you're not!

Be proud of who you are and appreciate your unique qualities; everyone is special in their own way.

Beautiful Water Lilies

Dominic the frog wasn't exactly a fashion model. In fact, his bumpy skin and wide eyes made him look more like a living olive than a pond superstar. But Dominic loved his lily pad. It was the best seat in the house for watching the sunset paint the sky in colors. One evening, as Dominic admired his favorite lily, Zelia, he puffed out his chest and said, "You know, Zelia, I would love to be a water lily just like you! You're so elegant, floating there like a fancy hat." Zelia, who secretly thought Dominic's bulging eyes were kind of funny, burst out laughing. "A water lily? You, Dominic? That's the silliest thing I've ever heard! You're about as graceful as a hopping sausage!"

Dominic's smile vanished along with his confidence. Zelia's words stung! He slunk away, feeling like all the joy had been sucked out of him. He was a green, lumpy, mistake of nature. Why was he even born? For days, Dominic hid under a leaf, avoiding Zelia and her sharp tongue. The pond wasn't much fun anymore. But then, something strange happened. The weather turned cold, and Zelia started looking less like a fancy hat and more like a wilted lettuce leaf. Her once-bright petals drooped, and her cheerful laughter faded.

Taking a deep breath, Dominic hopped over to Zelia. "Hey, Zelia," he croaked, "you don't look so good. Feeling a little less 'hat' and a little more 'sad sack' today?" Zelia sniffled. "The cold is awful, Dominic. It makes us lilies weak and wrinkly. We can't be beautiful forever, you know." Dominic stared at Zelia, then at the other wilting lilies. Maybe beauty wasn't everything. He looked at the sparkling frost on the leaves, the playful ripples on the water, even the warmth of his own bumpy green skin. The world was still full of cool stuff, even without perfectly perky flowers.

A few days later, Zelia, now looking like a soggy tissue, said, "Dominic, I owe you an apology. Being beautiful is nice, but it doesn't last. You, on the other hand, are always kind and fun, even when you look like a..." she paused, then whispered, "...a bumpy, yet adorable, olive." Dominic grinned. "Thanks, Zelia! Maybe being different isn't so bad after all." From then on, Dominic held his head high, bumpy skin and all. He learned that outer beauty, stuck around only as long as the flowers started to fade.

True beauty comes from kindness and how we treat others, not from how we look.

The Sun and the Wind

An old man trudged along the snowy road on a cold winter day, bundled like a burrito in his thick winter coat, eager to get home. Up above, the Sun and the Wind were having a heated argument about who was the strongest. "Strength isn't about how loud you roar," Mr. Sun boomed, his voice warm and cheerful.

Mr. Wind, a blustery fellow with a bad case of the puff-cheeks, scoffed. "Pish posh! Strength is about power! I can blow down houses!" "Oh yeah?" Mr. Sun chuckled. "Then how about a contest? Whoever makes Mr. Grady down there take off his coat first, wins!" Mr. Wind puffed himself up even bigger. "Easy peasy! I go first! Just watch!"

He charged down, howling like a furious dragon. He whipped the trees back and forth, flinging snow everywhere. Mr. Grady was freezing, thus gripped his coat tighter. The wind howled and huffed, but the colder it got, the more Mr. Grady wrapped himself up like a caterpillar in its cocoon. Mr. Wind, tired and out of puff, finally gave up. "Your turn, sunshine," he grumbled.

Mr. Sun peeked through the clouds and smiled. He didn't yell or blow, he just gently sent down warm rays. They melted the snowflakes on Mr. Grady's hat and tickled his face. Feeling the warmth creep in, Mr. Grady unbuttoned his coat, letting out a relieved sigh.

The sunbeams kept getting stronger, turning the chilly air into a cozy hug. Soon, Mr. Grady, with a big grin, slung his coat over his shoulder and continued his walk, feeling much happier. Mr. Sun winked at Mr. Wind. "See? Kindness is stronger than any bluster." Mr. Wind mumbled something about hot air balloons and gray clouds, but deep down, he knew the sun was right. Maybe true strength wasn't about being the loudest or meanest, but about making things a little warmer, a little brighter, just like a friendly smile on a cold winter day.

True strength lies in doing good deeds and being kind, not in using force.

Larry's Long Tail

Larry the lemur dashed into his house, slammed his school bag on the floor, and bolted to his room. He threw himself on the bed and started crying. His mom peeked in. "What's with all this drama, Larry?" she asked, her eyes full of concern. "School stinks!" he muttered, still crying uncontrollably. Larry told her about the mean jokes the other animals at school made about his long tail. "They always make fun of me, Mom," he said. "Today, because it was raining, they said they could use my tail to dry their laundry. They laughed and called me 'Laundry Tail' and 'Clothesline Larry.' They also say my tail looks like a fluffy mop and call me 'Mop Tail.' They even joked that I could use my tail to sweep the classroom floor and called me 'Broom Tail.' I don't want to go back to school ever again!"

His mom sat beside him, stroking his fur gently. "Those classmates sound like a bunch of bumbling baboons," she said. "Remember, Larry, your tail is what makes you, YOU! It's like your own personal swing, and the fluffiest fashion statement in the whole jungle!" Larry wasn't quite convinced. He spent the next few days hiding at home, pretending to be sick.

Then, one cold afternoon, the most terrifying thing happened! Hunters set a giant net trap in the jungle! Before Larry's classmates, even Mr. Mango the monkey teacher, could say "bananas" they were tangled up like flies in sticky syrup! Larry, playing nearby, saw the whole thing. His heart was racing. He had to do something! Without a moment's hesitation, Larry launched himself into action. Using his amazing, long tail like a jungle vine, he swung from tree to tree faster than a cheetah on roller skates. "Larry, you have to save us!" squeaked Tammy the turtle, upside down and wiggling her little legs. Larry landed next to the net. Using his strong hands and his tail for hanging from the tree branch, he untied the net.

The net dropped on the ground, and everyone tumbled out, a furry mess of relief. Mr. Mango looked at Larry. "Larry, you're a hero! Your amazing tail saved the day!" The other animals crowded around Larry. "We're so sorry for teasing you about your tail, Larry," Tammy mumbled. "It's the coolest tail ever!" Larry grinned, a happy feeling spreading through him. "It's okay," he chirped. "Just glad we're all safe." From that day on, Larry strutted back to school, his head held high, his tail swishing proudly. Being different wasn't a weakness, it was what made him extraordinary!

Our unique traits make us special, and sometimes, they can be our greatest strengths.

Orion's Big Day

Orion the parrot was feeling restless. Forget the boring "caw caw," Orion dreamed of human words. Every day, he would listen carefully as Mrs. Ramirez, his owner, greeted customers with a bright, "Good evening!" So, one day, POOF! Out came a perfect, "Good evening!" from Orion's shiny, black beak. The nearby cat, Maggy, nearly jumped out of her fur! Mrs. Ramirez was so proud of him. "Bravo, Orion! You did it!" Orion puffed up his chest, dreaming of fame. There was a big Bird Convention coming up, a place where birds showed off their coolest tricks. He just HAD to go and wow everyone!

At the convention, the park was a cacophony of chirps, tweets, and squawks. Nervous but excited, Orion landed near a group of chatty birds: a blue jay with a sassy voice, a red cardinal who looked like a superhero, a mockingbird who could copy any sound, and a wise old owl with big, round eyes. The blue jay spotted him first. "Hey there, feather ball! New in town?" Orion puffed up even more. "Good evening!" he squawked, proud as a peacock.

The other birds stopped chirping, their beaks agape. "Whoa!" chirped the cardinal. "A talking parrot! He knows the human language!" The mockingbird, who usually mimicked everyone, looked impressed. "I can only copy bird sounds, but you, Orion, you speak human!" Even the moody old owl hooted in approval. "Impressive, young one. Can you say anything else? Please, tell us!" Orion felt his feathers burning. He tried really hard to think of another word. But all that came out was another, loud, "Good evening!"

The other birds burst out laughing, wings flapping. The blue jay nudged him with her wing. "Hey, don't sweat it, buddy! One word is a great start!" The cardinal chirped, "Practice makes perfect! We all started somewhere, even Mr. Know-It-All owl here." The owl hooted and pretended to look offended. Orion relaxed a bit. Maybe he wasn't a master speaker yet, but he had made new friends! And learning more words sounded like a fun adventure. With a happy chirp, Orion joined the party, ready to practice his "Good evening" and learn some new words.

Enjoy and celebrate your achievements but know there is always room for improvement.

A Lie's Journey

One freezing winter day, in a village colder than any snowman's nose, a Lie was born. Unlike the usual gray Lies, this one shimmered with all the colors of the rainbow, promising happiness on planet Earth. Feeling like a superhero and curious about its powers, the Lie decided to explore the world. The first stop was the local school. The children went wild! They were captivated by its stories of a world without worries. The teachers marveled at its charm, and the headmaster was so impressed that he offered, "Stay here, and I will make you a vice principal!" The Lie considered the offer but grew restless very soon. It craved more attention and admiration, so it set off for the bustling market.

It marched to the village square, where everyone went crazy about it! The jewelers, bakers, and merchants all wanted it to stay. The jewelry maker, a kind woman with long fingers, said, "Stay with me, and I will make you golden bracelets." The baker, Mrs. Muffin-top, nearly fainted with joy – a happy world? "You can have all the cupcakes you want if you stay here," she said. The toymaker, Mr. Busbang, offered mountains of brand-new toys.

The Lie basked in the attention, but once again, it felt the urge to move on. It left the market and continued its journey down the road. There it bumped into a reporter, Nosey McAsky, who loved a juicy story more than anything. He interviewed the Lie and broadcasted it on TV and across the internet. The news spread fast, reaching every corner of the country.

Everyone went Lie-crazy! The mayor, a man so serious his tie never came off, wanted the Lie to stay forever. "We must make the Lie stay! It gives people hope," he exclaimed. Soon, even the president of the country heard about the Lie. The president, a wise and thoughtful leader, addressed the nation. "This Lie says that poverty, hunger, and war have vanished from the Earth. It was born a lie and will remain a lie, unless we all work together to make it true!" The Lie, wanted to bring happiness, but the president was right. It was up to everyone to make sure nobody was hungry or scared.

The youth of the country, inspired by the president's words, began to take action. They volunteered in their communities, helped those in need, and worked towards creating a better world. The kids got to organizing food drives and building playgrounds in poorer areas! The Lie realized then something incredible. Even though it started as a lie, it had inspired people to create a better world, with less hunger, less fear, and more kindness. It stopped wandering around and settled happily in the village, proud to be a part of something real, the efforts of the young people working to turn it into reality.

Hope can inspire positive change; you can become the change you want to see in this world.

Brave Little Eagles

High up in an oak tree taller than a skyscraper, two young eagles named Phoenix and Zen perched on a branch. They had just mastered the art of flapping without falling (mostly) and their parents swooped in with big news: "Time to catch your own lunch, squirts!" Phoenix, the braver of the two, puffed his chest out. "At last! I'm gonna snag the biggest, juiciest fish for lunch!" Zen, on the other hand, looked like he had just swallowed nails.

"Uh oh," he squeaked. "What if I fall? What if I can only catch soggy worms?" Phoenix nudged him with his wing. "Don't worry, little bro. The wind is like an invisible rope, holding you up!" Zen peered down at the ground, then back up at the fluffy white clouds. "But I don't see any rope..." Phoenix rolled his eyes. He was starting to get annoyed. "Zen, you've got your feathers, your enormous wings – the whole birdy package! Birds fly, that's what we do!"

With a confident screech, he launched himself off the branch, soaring through the air like a feathered arrow, riding invisible currents. Zen watched him disappear, his tummy going through a roller coaster. He knew he had to try, but his talons felt like jelly.

Taking a deep breath, he spread his wings and squeezed his eyes shut. "Okay, here goes nothing!" he mumbled, jumping into the open air. For a moment, Zen felt like he was falling fast. Panic squawked in his throat, but then... The wind whooshed under his wings, lifting him up! He peeked open one eye, then the other. The ground wasn't rushing up to meet him – he was actually flying! Zen squawked with delight! He swooped and dived, feeling lighter than a feather. "I'm flying! I'm really, truly flying!" he cried.

Then he spotted Phoenix in the distance, snatching a fish out of the river with a mighty splash. Zen puffed up with pride. He had faced his fear and discovered the awesome power of flight! He swooped down to join Phoenix, who grinned from beak to ear. "See, I knew you could do it!" Phoenix said. Zen landed next to him, feeling braver than a whole pack of lions. "Thanks, Phoenix. I just needed a little... nudge." The two eagles burst out laughing and took off together, ready to explore the world and catch lunch as a team.

Face your fears with courage, and you will discover just how strong and capable you really are.

Rainy Days

Rylee was a ray of sunshine with a contagious giggle. But there was one tiny gremlin in her world – the letter "R"! Whenever Rylee tried to say "rabbit," it came out a wobbly "wabbit," and "rainbow" transformed into a silly "wainbow." Rylee dreamed of a world with no "R"s at all! Inevitably, school wasn't always sunshine and lollipops for Rylee. Some kids, like Jake (who thought he was the funniest banana in the fruit basket), loved to tease. "Hey, Wylee," he would snicker, "do you want to play with my wabbit-eared stuffed animal?"

The other kids would laugh, making Rylee's cheeks turn red. Feeling quite depressed, Rylee stopped talking much. She would hide under the shade of the giant lemon tree in the schoolyard, watching the world go by with a sad frown. Every now and then, she would look up at the clouds, wondering if they ever got teased for their shapes.

One day, a pair of fluffy white clouds drifted over the school. They peeked down and saw Rylee all alone, looking like a lost puppy. "Why is she so sad?" one cloud asked the lemon tree. The lemon tree sighed its leaf-rustle sigh. "Those silly kids keep teasing Rylee because she says her 'R's' funny. She doesn't speak much now because of them!" The clouds puffed up with fury! Nobody messes with a sweet girl like Rylee. "We'll teach those rascals a lesson they won't forget," they grumbled to each other.

The next day, the teasing started again. As soon as Jake said, "Hey Wylee, is it going to wain today?" the sky opened up, like a watering can! A huge downpour drenched Jake and his friends, turning them into wet ducklings. The other kids shrieked and ran for cover, but every time they teased Rylee, the rain would start again, like a broken sprinkler! It didn't take long for them to catch on. "Maybe it rains every time we tease Rylee because it's not very nice?" Emily squeaked, shivering in her soaked clothes.

Jake scratched his head, finally understanding. "Yeah, maybe we should stop teasing her altogether." The next day, when Rylee walked by, there were no teases, just curious stares. Jake, as usual, stepped forward. "Rylee, we're very sorry for teasing you. It was mean, and we promise not to do it again." Rylee's eyes widened. "Weally?" she asked, surprised. Emily chimed in, "Really, Rylee. We're sorry." A huge smile bloomed on Rylee's face. And magically, it stopped raining on them. From that day on, nobody teased Rylee's "R"s anymore. She started talking more and more and whenever she sat under the lemon tree, it was with a joyful heart.

Be kind to others, and you will create a brighter, happier world for everyone.

The Island of Greed

Theodore, a fisherman with an unruly, long beard, clung to a splintered oar as his boat went belly-up in a fierce storm. After days of floating like a soggy pretzel, a wave plopped him onto a strange island. This island wasn't your typical vacation spot. The people here were as kind as a bunch of hungry hippos! They argued over everything, even a single fish!

On his first day on the island, Theodore witnessed two grown men chasing each other around the market, yelling about who saw it first. A lady swiped a mango from a little kid and walked away laughing proudly! Yikes! Theodore was a man with a big heart, so he decided to help these folks learn to share and care.

He started small. One day, he saw the two fish-fighters and said, "Ahoy, mateys! Why not share that fish, and I'll cook it up for everyone?" The men stared, surprised. At first, they grumbled, but seeing Theodore's friendly smile, they agreed. As they ate the yummy fish stew, they realized sharing was way better than crabby arguments. Next, Theodore spotted the mango-stealing lady. He walked over with a basket overflowing with juicy mangoes and said, "Here you go! And one extra for that little fella." The lady blinked, then a tiny smile peeked out. She shyly gave the extra mango to the kid, who grinned from ear to ear. "Thanks, mister!"

Another day, Theodore saw two kids wrestling over a shell. "What a neat treasure!" he said, kneeling. "Did you know that if you put it to your ear, you can hear the ocean roar?" He gave the shell to one of them, and the kids both listened, eyes wide open. They giggled as the seashell whispered secrets, forgetting all about fighting.

Slowly, Theodore's kindness spread. People started helping each other, sharing their food and tools, and laughing more! The island wasn't greedy anymore – it was a place filled with smiles and sunshine. One evening, the island's leader, a guy with a flowered shirt, walked up to Theodore. "Thanks for showing us how to be kind and work together," he said. "You're our island hero!" Theodore grinned, his heart full of warmth. "Sometimes," he said, "all it takes is a little bit of kindness to turn a frown upside down and make the world a friendlier place."

Kindness and cooperation can change people's hearts and maybe, eventually the world.

Drizzle Season

In Papertown, everything was like a giant, creative, art project! Houses were built from huge cardboard boxes, clothes were made from colorful tissues, and the people themselves were walking, talking paper cutouts! They loved reading stories in their paper libraries and writing silly poems on themselves with crayons. But there was one season that turned Papertown into a danger zone – Drizzle Season! Forget rainy days, in Papertown, the clouds rained... paperclips! Nasty, pointy paperclips that could give you a paper cut worse than reading a super boring book.

One gloomy morning, the sky turned gray, and Mayor Parchment, an old paper dude with a permanent crease down his forehead, said, "Citizens of Papertown! Drizzle Season is here! Run for cover!" The announcement sent shivers down everyone's papery spine. Drizzle Season meant danger, and fear hung heavy in the air. Everyone scrambled – paper teachers diving under desks, paper kids and their parents running frantically. A paper baker threw a flour sack down in frustration. "Just when I finished baking all those paper cupcakes!"

But Paige, a nice little girl, and her best friend Scribble, a walking graffiti masterpiece, were stuck playing tag in the park. Suddenly, a humongous paperclip came plummeting down like a pointy meteor! "Yikes!" yelped Paige as the clip snagged her arm, leaving a tear. Scribble, brave as always, grabbed Paige's hand. "Uh oh, papercut patrol to the rescue! We must get you to the Paper Hospital, pronto!" They raced through the storm, dodging the falling paperclips.

The hospital was overflowing with paper people; ripped elbows, torn knees, and even a few with paperclips stuck to their noses (ouch, that must have hurt)! Nurse Cardstock, a kind lady made from sturdy construction paper, rushed over. "Don't worry, Paige. We'll patch you up faster than you can say 'scissors.'" With a dab of special paper glue and a flower sticker, Paige's tear was history!

Meanwhile, Scribble was chatting with Doctor Origami, a master folder with a mustache. "Why can't we stop the paperclip rain?" he asked. Doctor Origami stroked his mustache. "Well, we can't change the weather, but we can be smarter! We can make sturdy umbrellas from wax paper and carry glue and sticker bandages everywhere we go!" From that day on, Papertown was better organized. Everyone had a mini-umbrella and a patch-up kit. The next paperclip drizzle came, but this time, Paige and Scribble stood cozy under their umbrellas, giggling as the paperclips bounced harmlessly off. Papertown wasn't scared of Drizzle Season anymore - they were ready for it.

Being prepared ahead of time can help you handle any challenge that comes your way.

Maisie and Tassy

Maisie the Mouse had a nose for adventure as twitchy as her whiskers. She lived by a wide, gurgling river, enjoying every moment of it. It was peaceful and away from danger - just what a mouse needed. One cold day, she longed to explore the other side, but the water whooshed by, way too fast for her tiny legs! Just then, Tassy the Turtle lumbered by. Tassy was as wise as an owl and moved at the speed of... well, a turtle.

"Hey, Tassy!" squeaked Maisie. "Think you could give a small adventurer like me a lift across?" Tassy winked with one sleepy eye. "Hop on, little sprout! My shell's always open for friends." Maisie scrambled onto Tassy's back, feeling safe and cozy on her broad, comfortable roof. Tassy paddled with strong, slow strokes, dodging playful fish along the way.

When they reached the other side, Maisie hopped off, her whiskers twitching with excitement. "Thank you so much, Tassy!" she squeaked. "I owe you one! How about a lifetime supply of the best cheese?" Tassy chuckled. "No fancy cheese for me, Maisie. But as winter approaches, I'll be snoozing more than usual. Maybe you could pop by and say hi sometimes? I would appreciate the company." "You got it!" squeaked Maisie, bouncing with excitement.

As the leaves turned crunchy, and the air turned cooler, Tassy slowed down to a sleepy crawl. She spent most days curled up under a rock. But just like she promised, Maisie visited often. She would bring Tassy yummy treats – acorns, juicy berries, and even a teensy bit of cheese! One extra-chilly afternoon, Maisie scurried over with a pile of yummy leaves and a stash of nuts. "Hibernation hotel open for business!" she squeaked.

Tassy cracked one eye open. "Hey there, little friend. Thanks for the treats! Your visits always brighten my day." Maisie snuggled beside Tassy, sharing stories of her daring escapes from hungry owls and her delicious discoveries in the bakery next door (don't tell the baker)!

They both realized how much they cherished these visits. Winter dragged on, but Maisie never missed a day. Tassy was cozy and well-fed, and Maisie learned the true meaning of friendship. Finally, spring peeped over the horizon. Tassy stretched her legs and basked in the sunshine. "Spring is here, Maisie! Thanks for being the best winter buddy ever!" "Anytime, Tassy! I learned a ton about friendship and keeping warm with good company," Maisie said. Tassy smiled. She knew that true friends stick together, no matter how cold or hot things get.

True friendship means being there for each other, especially when times are tough.

The Curious Deer

Daisy the deer was a walking question mark. Unlike her mama, Grace (calm as a cucumber), and the other grown-up deer, Daisy couldn't resist a good mystery. One cold, winter morning, while playing hide-and-seek with the squirrels, Daisy spotted something that made her eyes bug out bigger than blueberries. Beyond the familiar trees lay a meadow covered in snow! It looked like a delicious birthday cake frosted with sugar. "Oooh, got to check that out!" she thought, her hooves already itching to run.

Just as she was about to leapfrog a bush and head for the meadow, Luca the old deer, stopped her with a hoof raised. "Whoa there, Daisy! Where's the fire?" "Fire? There's no fire, Luca," Daisy giggled. "Just that meadow over there. It looks like a yummy sugar pot! I just have to check it out." Luca sighed. "That meadow, Daisy, belongs to the humans. And humans, well, they're not big fans of deer visitors. They set sneaky traps that can grab you tight and make you scream for dear life!"

Daisy's ears drooped. "But it looks like so much fun! I'll just peek for a sec, I promise! I'll be extra careful!" Luca knew that look. It was the "I-won't-get-caught" look that usually ended in trouble. "Daisy," he pleaded, "the shiny things might look fun, but trust me, they're not worth getting stuck in." But curiosity was a powerful itch, and when Luca turned away for a second, Daisy was off!

In the meadow, she found a sparkly thing that looked suspiciously like a fancy button! Suddenly, the world turned ouch-y. A sneaky trap had clamped onto Daisy's leg, holding her tight. "Heeelp!" she cried, tears welling up in her big, brown eyes. Back in the forest, Luca heard Daisy's cry and knew exactly what had happened. He rallied the other deer, and soon, Mama Grace was a frantic mess. "We have to save her!" she cried. Using their antlers and hooves like super tools, the deer family worked together. They pried open the trap and freed Daisy, who could barely walk.

Back in the safe shade of the trees, Daisy hung her head low. "I'm so sorry," she mumbled. "I should have listened." Mama Grace nuzzled her gently. "We're just happy you're safe, sweetie. But remember, rules aren't there to stop your fun, they're there to keep you safe." Luca winked. "Curiosity is great, Daisy, but sometimes, listening to those who care about you is even better." From that day on, Daisy still explored the forest, but she always kept a safe distance from the meadow and its shiny surprises.

Rules have been made for a reason; understanding them, can keep you safe from harm.

The Olympic Dream

Isaac the lion lived in the heart of the savanna. Isaac wasn't just any lion, though! Isaac dreamed of big things – like winning the gold medal at the Winter Animal Olympics, in the 100-meter dash! The problem was, Isaac trained like a wild thing, chasing zebras all day, but he couldn't seem to get fast enough. One day, while Isaac was practicing (and failing) to outrun an outstandingly fast warthog, Cheetah Coach, the savanna's fastest sprinter, trotted by.

"Hey Isaac," he said, with a cheetah grin. "Training hard, but looking a little... well, sluggish." Isaac puffed out his chest, sending a cloud of dust flying. "Me? Slow? Never! I eat the strongest meat, the biggest eggs – I'm practically a walking power-burger!" Cheetah Coach chuckled. "Isaac, there's more to being fast than just... meat-breath. You have to fuel your body right, like a race car needs the best gas!" Isaac tilted his head, confused. "Fuel my body? You mean with more meat?"

Cheetah Coach shook his head. "Nope! Think rainbow colors! Fruits, veggies, grains – all that good stuff gives you the energy you need to win. Plus, rest! Your muscles have to recharge, just like your phone after too many funny animal videos!" Isaac's eyes widened. Rainbow food and naps? This winning thing might be harder than he thought. But Isaac was determined. He started chewing on juicy berries, munching on crunchy carrots, and even tried a few (okay, maybe a lot) of nuts and seeds. As it turns out, squirrels hoard the best snacks! He also made sure to take long naps under his favorite shady baobab tree.

Finally, the Winter Animal Olympics arrived! Isaac, feeling lighter than a feather and stronger than a pride of lions, stood at the starting line. The crowd cheered on, the air was crisp, and his tummy was full of healthy cheetah-approved fuel. "Ready, set, go!" the announcer roared. Isaac bolted! He was a blur of fur and muscle, leaving other animals in his dust!

As he crossed the finish line first, the crowd went wild, making him feel so proud! Cheetah Coach, with a wide grin reaching his ears, congratulated Isaac. "You did it, champ! Remember, winning isn't just about running fast, it's about taking care of yourself too." Isaac, munching on his gold medal (not really, those are for biting), smiled. He learned that the key to winning wasn't just how hard you trained, but how well you treated your body – with good food, enough sleep, and maybe even a few more naps under a shady tree.

Success comes from a balanced approach; taking care of your body helps you achieve your dreams.

Dwarf Village

Deep in the frosted land of Dwarfwood, where icicles hung like crystal fangs, lived a bunch of quirky dwarfs. Snibble, was the fastest fish gatherer in the whole village. Blinny, strong as a tiny ox, could build anything out of ice and snow – from furniture to enormous snow-castles! Then there was Loodle, small but with a big heart. These three friends were awesome, but sometimes, they felt like a band of misfits – a little different from the cooler crowd. The most popular dwarfs, led by Sparkle (who always seemed to have a fresh layer of glitter on her nose), set the trends. They wore fancy snowflake necklaces and spoke in a language that sounded mostly like gibberish to everyone else.

One snowy afternoon, huddled in their cozy ice cave, Snibble sighed. "I wish we could be cool like Sparkle and her gang," he said fiddling with a plain wooden bead around his neck. Blinny thumped his leg against the ice floor, making a soft thud. "Yeah, they seem to have all the fun. We're just... different." Loodle, always the optimist, squeaked, "Maybe we can make our own snowflake necklaces and learn their silly talk! Then they'll want to be friends with us." So, the three friends got to work. They strung sparkling ice crystals on a thread and practiced their "cool" talk, which mostly involved saying "epic" after everything. "This ice cave is epic!" or "Those cookies were epic!" As it turns out, everything can be epic when you say it enough.

Feeling totally epic (and a little silly), they marched over to Sparkle and her friends. But instead of high-fives, all they got was giggles and eye rolls. "Uh, nice try, weirdos," Sparkle snickered. "You can't just copy us to be cool." Dejected, the three friends slunk back to their cave. "I guess we'll never be like them," Blinny mumbled, feeling sad.

Suddenly, a voice was heard from the doorway. It was Frostina, an old dwarf lady. "Why do you want to be like them?" she said softly. "You each have amazing talents! True friends will love you for who you are, not for having some fancy necklace." Frostina's words were like a warm fire on a chilly day. Snibble, Blinny, and Loodle decided to forget about fitting in and instead, focus on what made them special.

Snibble organized a fun race through the snowy forest, Blinny built a big ice dragon that roared smoke (not really), and Loodle led the entire village in a heartwarming song that made everyone sing along. Everyone loved their unique ideas, and even Sparkle and her friends joined in the fun. They finally realized that being cool wasn't about copying each other, but celebrating how awesome everyone was in their own special way. The three friends learned that the coolest thing you can ever be, is yourself, and true friends will love you for all your weird, yet wonderful quirks!

True friends accept and appreciate you for who you really are and celebrate your unique qualities.

A Boy and a Tree

Mike wasn't just any average backyard explorer. Sure, he liked building forts out of sticks and leaves, and chasing butterflies, but his most prized discovery was a tiny, twiggy sprout peeking out from the dirt. "Whoa, a baby tree!" Mike exclaimed, his eyes wide with wonder. This wasn't just any tree, though. This was going to become Mike's best friend. He named it Walnut, because, well, it was a walnut tree, and every morning, he would be out there with his watering can, giving Walnut a big drink.

Walnut, being a tree, couldn't exactly reply to Mike's words, but its leaves would wiggle in a happy dance. Year after year, Walnut grew taller, its branches stretching towards the sky. Mike grew taller too, no longer the little watering-can kid. Now a teenager, Mike loved hanging out under Walnut's cool shade. He would curl up with a book or just lie there, watching the white clouds drift by. "Thanks for being the best friend ever, Walnut," he would say, giving the trunk a friendly thump. "You're always there for me, even when I have homework headaches."

One day, something amazing happened! Walnut sprouted a bunch of bumpy green balls. "Look, Mike!" its leaves seemed to whisper. "I made a present for you!" Mike's eyes widened. These weren't just any balls; they were walnuts! He carefully cracked one open, revealing a delicious, wrinkly treasure inside. "Wow, Walnut, these are awesome!" he exclaimed.

Years flew by, and Walnut kept growing. Not only did it give Mike yummy snacks, but its branches grew so strong, they could be used to build things! When Mike's old table broke, he had an idea. "Hey, Walnut," he said, looking up at the giant tree. "Would you mind if I borrowed a few of your branches to build a new table? I promise I'll only take what I need, and you'll still be the coolest tree on the block!" The wind rustled through Walnut's leaves, almost making them nod "Yes." Mike carefully snipped a few branches, and soon, he made a brand-new, sturdy table. "You're the best tree ever, Walnut," Mike said, patting the smooth wood. "Don't worry, I'll always take care of you."

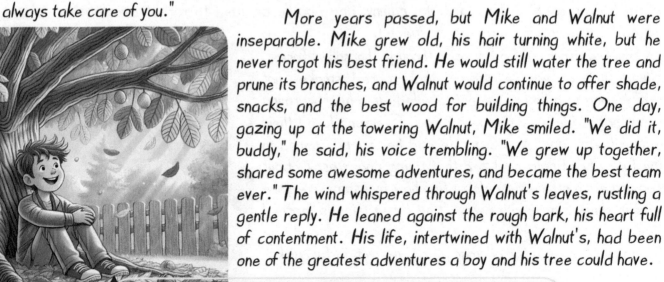

More years passed, but Mike and Walnut were inseparable. Mike grew old, his hair turning white, but he never forgot his best friend. He would still water the tree and prune its branches, and Walnut would continue to offer shade, snacks, and the best wood for building things. One day, gazing up at the towering Walnut, Mike smiled. "We did it, buddy," he said, his voice trembling. "We grew up together, shared some awesome adventures, and became the best team ever." The wind whispered through Walnut's leaves, rustling a gentle reply. He leaned against the rough bark, his heart full of contentment. His life, intertwined with Walnut's, had been one of the greatest adventures a boy and his tree could have.

Living in harmony with nature can be very rewarding, offering a life full of mutual support.

A Snowman's Tale

On a crisp winter morning, I came to life. It all began when the boy and the girl arrived, rosy cheeks from the cold, carrying bundles of joy in their mitten-clad hands. The boy, with a laugh that could wake a sleeping bear, scooped up a pile of snow. "Time to build a friend!" he said. The girl, her bright scarf a rainbow against the white, started rolling the snow into big snowballs. First, a large one went on the bottom – my super strong foundation! "This is where my awesome snow body will begin," I thought.

Next, a slightly smaller snowball became my belly. I could practically feel their careful hands smoothing out my lumps. "Almost there!" I thought, getting all excited. Finally, the tiniest snowball got plopped on top – my head! "There you go, buddy," the girl giggled. The boy reached into his pocket and pulled out... two shiny black buttons! He stuck them right on my face. "Woah, cool! These must be my eyes," I thought, blinking my brand-new button eyes open for the first time. The world looked kind of wonky, but hey, at least I could see!

The girl wasn't done yet. She whipped out a bright orange carrot and shoved it right in the middle of my face. "A nose? You have got to be kidding me," I thought, but deep down, I kind of liked it. It gave me character! For my smile, they made a row of small pebbles. They weren't perfect, but hey, a quirky smile is better than no smile at all, right? Plus, the kids were grinning from ear to ear, so I figured I should join the fun. The boy even put a fuzzy hat on my head and the girl wrapped a colorful scarf around my neck! I wasn't sure what to hold, but the kids found two sticks and stuck them in my sides for arms. "Maybe I can use them to scratch my... I guess I don't have an itch," I thought.

Finally, they added a row of buttons down my front – the finishing touch! I thought they had done a great job. The kids danced around me, their laughter warming me more than any hat ever could. I couldn't exactly high-five them back, but trust me, I was having a blast! I knew the sunshine might melt me away tomorrow, but for now, I soaked up their friendship and the joy of being a snowman. As the sun began to set, the kids waved goodbye. "See you tomorrow, buddy!" the boy yelled. I stood tall and proud, a frosty friend forever in their hearts!

Enjoy the company of good friends and cherish the happy memories you create with them.

The Fish Council

Deep down in the freezing Antarctic Ocean, Silvy the silverfish was having so much fun! Zipping through the crystal-clear water, her scales shimmered under the dim light. But her fin stopped flapping when she saw Icy the icefish. Icy, usually the coolest dude around, looked like he had swallowed a rotten fish. "Hey Icy, what's wrong?" Silvy asked, her voice full of concern. "You look like you just met an enormous whale with bad breath!"

Icy sighed, his see-through body turning even paler. "Ugh, it's those human guys again, Silvy. They keep going around in their noisy boats, trying to catch us fish for who-knows-what reason!" Silvy's eyes widened. "Catch us? Like, for a big fish-stick sandwich?" Icy shivered. "Almost! Last week, a humongous net scooped up a bunch of my friends! I barely escaped by squeezing through a hole!" Silvy gasped. "Yikes! I almost got tricked too! These humans dangle shiny hooks that look like yummy treats, but they're actually traps! Luckily, I noticed the metal and bolted faster than a penguin on roller skates!" Icy shook his head. "They don't seem to understand they're messing with our way of life! We have to do something, Silvy!"

Silvy, always the quick thinker, perked up. "We can't just hide forever! Let's call a fish meeting – a fin summit, if you will! We'll invite fish from all the oceans – the colorful coral reefs, the seaweed forests, the whole gang!" Icy's eyes sparkled. "Brilliant, Silvy! But how do we spread the word across the whole big ocean?" Silvy winked. "Leave that to me! My jellyfish friends are the ultimate gossip – they spread news faster than a barracuda chases sardines! We'll get fish from all corners swimming our way in no time!"

And so, Silvy sent out her fishy invitations through the ocean currents. Soon, the news reached every fin and tentacle. A week later, under the shimmering ice, an assembly, unlike any other took place! Fish of all shapes and sizes – from goofy puffers to wise old sea turtles – gathered to discuss how to deal with the human problem.

Silvy, addressed the crowd. "Fish friends! We have to work together to protect our underwater world! By joining flippers, we can find a way to live without constantly worrying, fishy-style!" Ideas splashed around. Some fish suggested teaching humans about sustainable fishing, while others wanted to create special fish-only zones, where no boats could go, to protect the endangered species! With all their brilliant minds working together, they formed a plan to protect their fishy homes and keep the ocean safe for everyone. As the meeting ended, Silvy and Icy knew the fight was not over, but they weren't alone anymore.

Working together to find solutions can help overcome even the greatest challenges.

Mathew's Melody

Matthew was different than most kids. He was born with one leg shorter than the other. This meant getting around was a bit of a challenge, and sometimes kids could be... well, not very kind. "Hey, look at Matthew!" they would shout. "He walks like a cat with two left feet!" These taunts stung like a swarm of angry bees, and Matthew would retreat to his room, feeling very lonely. But Matthew had a secret weapon – music! Surrounded by shiny instruments in his room, he would play the piano, strum the guitar, and even invent silly songs. Music was his magical world, where nobody cared if he walked funny.

One day, as Matthew was tinkling out a sad tune on the piano, his old neighbor, Mr. Harry stopped by. Mr. Harry had heard the beautiful music floating out the window. He knew right away that Matthew had a special talent hidden inside him, just waiting to be unleashed! "Hey there, Matthew," he said, with a kind voice. "That music is incredible! You've got the magic touch!" Matthew peeked up, surprised but feeling a flicker of sunshine in his heart. "Thanks, Mr. Harry. Music makes me forget the teasing... for a while, anyway."

Mr. Harry smiled. "Music is like a magical portal to a different world, Matthew! It can make you feel brave and strong. I used to be a music teacher. How about I help you become a musician too?" Eyes wide with excitement, Matthew practically shouted, "Yes please!" From then on, Mr. Harry became Matthew's music guru. They practiced for hours, turning all of Matthew's feelings – the sad ones, the happy ones, and even the "those-kids-are-being-mean" ones – into beautiful melodies.

One afternoon, the school announced a talent show. Matthew wanted to participate but he felt anxious about performing in front of everyone. But Mr. Harry, his biggest fan, insisted, "Go for it, Matthew! Let your music do the talking!"

On the big night, Matthew stood backstage, all nervous. But as his fingers touched the piano keys, he remembered all the hard work and the magic of music. The first note filled the room, then another, and soon the whole auditorium was quiet, listening to Matthew's amazing story told through music. When the last note faded, there was a stunned silence, followed by an eruption of applause that almost shook the roof off! Even the kids who used to tease him were cheering, their eyes filled with awe. Matthew realized that his love for music wasn't just a secret weapon – it was his superpower! A newfound confidence was warming him from the inside out.

Follow your dreams and let them guide you; don't let others judge your future or your dreams.

Shelly's Discovery

Shelly the snail was about as fast as a sleepy sloth on a snooze break. But that didn't bother Shelly. She loved her slow and peaceful life, munching on crunchy leaves and taking long naps under sparkly snowflakes. The only problem? Shelly was shy as a blushing ladybug. Talking, especially to other garden creatures, made her clam up tighter than her own shell.

One winter day, Shelly was enjoying a frozen salad (don't knock it till you try it) when a group of noisy insects buzzed by. Benny the Beetle, the garden's self-proclaimed "king of cool," spotted Shelly. "Hey look, it's Shelly the Slowpoke! Taking a leisurely stroll, are we?" he said, with a laughter that sounded just plain mean. Shelly felt her cheeks turn red, immediately tucking herself into her shell. She wished she could burrow underground and build a cozy fort of leaves. The other insects giggled, making Shelly want to disappear even more.

For days, Shelly stuck to the shadows of the garden, avoiding the main paths where the other creatures hung out. She would rather be alone than endure their teasing. But one very chilly morning, as Shelly explored a quiet, snowy corner, she saw something unbelievable. A tiny little mouse, no bigger than a button, was facing off against a huge, fierce-looking cat! The mouse squeaked bravely, even though it trembled. "You might be a giant fuzzball," it squeaked, "but that doesn't mean you can scare me!" The cat, surprised by the mouse's moxie, slowly backed away, its tail between its legs. Shelly watched in awe as the tiny mouse scurried off, its little chest puffed out with pride.

That day, Shelly learned a big lesson. Bravery wasn't about how big you were, it was about how brave you felt inside! The next day, she came across Benny the Beetle again. He opened his mouth to fire another rude comment, but this time, Shelly stopped him. Taking a deep breath, she said (in a voice much braver than she felt), "Benny, that's not very nice. We all have our special talents, and mine happens to be taking it easy!"

Benny blinked, surprised. "I... I wasn't trying to be mean," he stammered. Shelly continued, her voice a little stronger now. "Let's all be nice to each other, okay?" The other insects, who had gathered around to watch, looked at Shelly with newfound respect. Even Benny mumbled an apology (which kind of sounded like "sorry-not-sorry," but hey, it was a start). From that day on, Shelly wasn't just the quiet snail anymore. Benny even learned to be respectful (most of the time), and winter, which once felt cold and lonely, blossomed into a season of warmth and friendship for Shelly.

Believe in yourself and find the courage to speak up; your voice has the power to make a difference.

Gemma and Kaylee

Gemma and Kaylee were the ultimate best friends. They stuck together like peanut butter and jelly, sharing secrets, giggling like hyenas, and always having each other's backs. However, one rainy afternoon in class, Gemma witnessed something that made her frown. Kaylee, who was sitting next to Ben, did a ninja-move hand swipe and yanked his pencil right off his desk faster than you could say "borrowing"! "Kaylee, that wasn't cool," Gemma whispered during recess. "Why did you take Ben's pencil?" Kaylee shrugged, twirling the pencil like a tiny baton. "It's just a pencil, Gem. He has, like, a whole forest of them."

Gemma wasn't convinced. Stealing, even something small, felt bad. She decided to teach Kaylee a lesson, a very important lesson. That weekend, Gemma had a sleepover at Kaylee's house. They built a tall, blanket fort, munched on popcorn, and watched movies filled with silly superheroes. Finally, bedtime rolled around. As Gemma snuggled into her sleeping bag, she spotted Kaylee's most prized possession – Mr. Cuddles, her soft, lovey teddy bear that had been with her since she was a tiny baby. Gemma knew how much that bear meant to Kaylee.

When Kaylee went downstairs to get some yummy snacks, Gemma did something that made her feel bad, but it was for a good cause. She secretly stashed Mr. Cuddles in her backpack! The next day at school, Kaylee looked depressed. "Gemma, I can't find Mr. Cuddles anywhere!" she cried, her eyes welling up with tears. "I looked under my bed, behind the couch, even in the toilet (don't ask)!" Gemma felt a pang of guilt, but she knew this was part of the plan. Taking a deep breath, she asked softly, "How does it feel to lose something important, Kaylee? Maybe a little like Ben felt when his pencil disappeared?" Kaylee's eyes widened like saucers. She felt guilty.

"Oh no," she mumbled, "I didn't think about it like that. It's awful to lose something you love!" Seeing her friend's regret, Gemma knew it was time to confess. With a grin, she dug into her backpack and pulled out Mr. Cuddles! Relief flooded Kaylee's face as she hugged her teddy bear tight. "Gemma, I'm so sorry! I shouldn't have taken Ben's pencil. I'll give it back and apologize right away!" True to her word, Kaylee returned the pencil to Ben, with a big apology. From that day on, Kaylee never forgot the importance of asking nicely to borrow something and respecting other people's belongings.

Respect others' belongings and understand their feelings; even small actions can have a big impact.

A New Chapter

Snowflakes swirled outside like a million tiny ballerinas as Mark and Skylar sat on the couch, all cozy and warm. But inside them, things weren't quite so cheerful. Mom and Dad had a serious look on their faces, like they were about to announce some terrible news. "There's something we need to tell you," Dad began, his voice low. "Your awesome Dad," (he winked) "got offered an amazing job in a totally new town!" Mark's jaw dropped and Skylar's eyes welled up. "But... but what about our friends?" she squeaked. "And what about Christmas? We can't just skip Christmas!" Mom hugged her. "We know, honey. We love our house here too, but this new job is like a golden ticket for Dad – it'll help our family a lot."

The next few days were a whirlwind of packing boxes and tearful goodbyes. Mark and Skylar hugged their friends goodbye, feeling as if they would never see them again. On their last night, they had a big holiday party with all the neighbors. They tried to be happy, but leaving their house felt like leaving the life they had known forever. Moving day arrived, and snow covered everything in a white blanket. Mark snuck a last peek at his old house, his throat tightening like wearing a too-small scarf. "Goodbye, home," he mumbled. The drive to the new town was long. Mark and Skylar stared out the window, their faces all depressed.

Finally, they pulled up to a new house that looked to their eyes like a big question mark. Boxes were piled everywhere, and the rooms felt empty and echoey. That night, Mom tried to cheer them up. "How about decorating a spectacular Christmas tree?" she said. They unpacked the ornaments, some sparkly, some shaped like funny animals. Slowly, the house started to feel a little less gloomy.

The next day, Mark and Skylar explored their new neighborhood. They found a park with a monstrous hill, perfect for epic sledding adventures. As they whooshed down the hill, their laughter echoed through the air, chasing away the sad feelings for a while. Soon, they met some kids who lived nearby. John, a boy with a wide smile, invited them to a holiday party. Mark and Skylar weren't sure, but their parents gave them a gentle push.

The party was fantastic, with games, yummy treats, and even a cute, little cat in a Santa hat! On Christmas Eve, they all gathered around their new Christmas tree. The house might not have felt exactly like home yet, but being together filled it with a warm, fuzzy feeling. Mark nudged Skylar and whispered, "Maybe this new place won't be so bad after all." Skylar grinned. "Yeah, we can make new friends and have new adventures. Besides, there's always next year for the big teddy bear rescue mission at our old house!" They both laughed, the spirit of Christmas filling them, no matter where they were.

Home is where your family is, and new beginnings can bring new joys and cherished memories.

A Superhero's Tale

Hey there, my name is Wavy, your average, everyday drop of water. But hold onto your fins, because I'm about to tell you how I became a Water Superhero! It all started way up high, in a big fluffy cloud. That's where I was born, just a speck among a million others. Then, one windy day, the whole cloud... sneezed and we all tumbled down as raindrops! It was like the coolest water slide ever, whooshing past white clouds and traveling towards the ground. We landed with a splash in a sparkling mountain stream, and off I went on an adventure! I gurgled with my fellow water drops, winding through twisty forests and tickling the toes of happy flowers.

Finally, we reached a busy town filled with honking horns and buildings that scraped the sky. In this town lived a nice girl named Mila. Mila was kind and curious, always asking questions like, "Why is the sky blue?" and "Do fish wear tiny hats?" The answer is no by the way, in case you were wondering. One day, I found myself on a mission: a cleaning mission! Mila was brushing her teeth, but she left the faucet running while doing it. All that water going to waste! I wished I could shout, "Please, close that faucet! Don't you know I could be watering a thirsty sunflower?"

Later that night, I was part of a big shower for Mila. She was singing a happy tune, but the shower seemed to last forever! "Ugh, if only she knew how precious I am," I sighed. That's when a super idea bubbled up in me! I would become a Water Superhero, teaching everyone to save water! The next day, I hitched a ride on a warm sunbeam and evaporated back into the sky, rejoining my cloud family. Together, we floated over Mila's town, ready to spread our wisdom. When it rained next, Mila put a bucket outside to catch us. "Good thinking, Mila!" I splashed happily. Mila's very smart grandma showed her how to use the rainwater to water the plants. I felt a tingle of pride – every drop saved made a difference!

Finally, my chance came! As Mila stood by the ocean, I gathered all my courage and whispered through the waves, "Hi, Mila! Thanks for saving me! But here's the secret code for Water Superheroes: short showers, turn off the faucet when you brush your teeth and always be on the lookout for ways to save water!" Mila's eyes got big and round. "I understand, Wavy! I'll be a Water Superhero too!" she promised. And that's how it all started! With Mila's help, the word spread. Soon, everyone was saving water – Mila's friends, her family, the whole town! They all became Water Superheroes, protecting me and making sure I could keep on helping others. Now, here I am, part of the big, blue ocean, feeling pretty awesome. We may be just tiny drops, but together, we can make a big splash!

✦ Be a Water Superhero; small actions to save water make a big difference. ✦

The Christmas Tree

Chaos erupted in the Carson living room! Tinsel rained down like festive snow, and a rogue ornament soared across the room, narrowly missing Mr. Carson's head. "Careful, Bonnie!" shrieked Mason, dodging a sparkly avalanche. "We're just trying to decorate!" Bonnie protested with a bauble tangled in her hair. Their parents, Mr. and Mrs. Carson, chuckled.

They were used to the annual Christmas tree decorating war zone. "Alright, alright," shouted Mr. Carson, holding up his hands. "Let's remember, Christmas isn't just about the tinsel tornado we seem to be creating." Mrs. Carson winked. "Exactly, honey. It's about the story of the first Christmas, way back when."

Mason's eyes widened. "Storytime! Storytime!" he chanted, bouncing on the sofa. Bonnie, untangling herself from the tinsel, settled in with a dramatic sigh. "So," Mrs. Carson began, "imagine Mary and Joseph on the road with a very important baby on the way. But when they reached Bethlehem they were unable to find shelter for the night, so they ended up in a stable – basically a barn for animals." Mason scrunched up his nose. "A barn? Jesus was born in a barn?" "Hey, it wasn't that bad," Mrs. Carson explained with a grin. "The cows and sheep helped keep the baby warm with their fuzzy breaths!" Bonnie giggled. "We learned that at school yesterday!"

Mr. Carson took over the story. "But seriously, kids," he said, "although baby Jesus was born in a stable, it was the most special night ever. It reminds us that Christmas is about love and family, not fancy stuff." Mason pointed at a mountain of presents under the tree. "But presents are fun too, right?" "Of course!" Mrs. Carson agreed. "But still, the best gifts are the ones you give from the heart, like that time you made cookies for Mrs. Parker next door."

Mason grinned. "Those cookies were awesome... almost as awesome as the time we donated a big stuffed bear to the animal shelter!" Bonnie added, "Yeah, the puppies loved it!" As they finished decorating the tree, fairy lights twinkling merrily, a warm feeling filled the room. It wasn't just the Christmas spirit (although that helped), it was the feeling of being together, a family wrapped in love and laughter. Maybe their Christmas tree did look a bit like a glitter bomb went off, but hey, that was just their style. After all, the most important things about Christmas weren't perfect decorations, but the messy, joyful memories they made together.

Christmas is about love, humility, and kindness, not the material gifts we receive.

A Christmas Dream

Jason shivered under his mountain of blankets. "Goodnight, Mom," he mumbled, barely keeping his eyes open. Mom tucked him in extra tight. "Sweet dreams, my little angel," she whispered. As soon as he closed his eyes, Jason suddenly wasn't in his bed anymore! He was floating in the sky, flying over a tiny village! Below, he spotted a confused couple – a young lady with a worried frown on her face, riding a donkey, and a man with a heavy backpack.

"Whoa, where am I?" Jason whispered. He swooped down closer, to see better. "We have to find a place to stay, Joseph," the poor lady said. "The baby is coming any minute!" Joseph sighed. They knocked on doors all over town, but everywhere they went, the answer was the same: "Sorry, no vacancy!" Jason felt compassion for them. They had to find a warm place to spend the night. Finally, they reached the edge of town. There, nestled among piles of hay, was a stable full of mooing cows and snoozing sheep. "This will have to do," Joseph decided.

He helped the lady, Mary, down from the donkey and made her a cozy bed of hay. Jason peeked inside – it wasn't exactly a five-star hotel, but it was warm and cozy, thanks to all the fluffy animals. Then, a bright light filled the stable. Jason gasped. A bright, otherworldly star twinkled overhead, bathing everything in a golden glow. Winged angels floated down, singing a joyful tune that sounded like Christmas carols. "Whoa, are those... real angels?" Jason whispered. Mom would love to see this! The angels landed around the manger, singing happily. Humble shepherds walked in, bringing tiny gifts to the newborn baby. "This baby," said one shepherd, holding up a squirming lamb, "is here to teach us kindness and humility..."

Slowly, the dream faded, and Jason woke up with a smile on his face. He raced to his mom, babbling about singing angels and a super bright star. Mom hugged him tight. "Sounds like a magical dream, honey. Remember, Christmas is all about love and kindness, just like the baby you saw." Jason nodded, understanding dawning on him like a sunrise. Christmas wasn't just about presents (although those were awesome too). It was about being kind, sharing with others, and maybe even making friends with some singing angels! Now that was a Christmas adventure!

The true spirit of Christmas lies in love, kindness, and humility, just as Jesus taught us.

The First Christmas

A long time ago, in a quiet town named Bethlehem, a journey stretched wearisome for Joseph and Mary. Mary, soon to welcome a baby, needed rest. Sadly, every cozy inn they visited had a sign that read "No vacancy!" Joseph's heart sank, but a kind innkeeper, wanting to help them, offered a spot in his stable! It wasn't fancy, with hay for a bed and animal friends nearby, but it was warm and safe.

That night, beneath a sky sparkling with the brightest star ever seen, Mary gave birth to a precious baby boy. They named him Jesus. Out in the fields, shepherds kept watch over their sheep. It wasn't the most exciting job, but it was important! Suddenly, a light brighter than a thousand flashlights filled the sky. A dazzling angel with wings that shimmered like snowflakes appeared before them. The shepherds, wide-eyed and terrified, froze! "Don't be afraid!" said the angel in a gentle voice. "I bring you good news! A special baby, a special king, was just born in the nearby town of Bethlehem. Go find him! He's wrapped up in a cozy manger for the animals, inside a humble stable."

Then, the sky filled with even more angels, singing a beautiful melody - joyful Christmas carols. "Sing praises to God!" they sang, "Peace on Earth for everyone!" The shepherds, hearts full of wonder, raced down the hill, leaving their sleepy sheep behind for a little while. Inside the stable, they found Mary and Joseph, glowing with love for their new baby. And there, nestled among the hay, was baby Jesus.

The shepherds kneeled, feeling that they had just met a real-life savior. This little baby came on Earth to spread love and kindness, just like the twinkling star above! Mary smiled warmly, touched by their visit. The shepherds left, sharing the news of the angels and the baby with everyone they met. Everyone they talked to felt a sense of wonder, as they showed their faith and respect for the newborn king. The shepherds skipped back to their sheep, forever changed by the most magical night ever. They knew, deep down, that baby Jesus was something special, and they couldn't wait to see the good things he would bring to this world!

The birth of Jesus teaches us about love, hope, and being kind to others.

Three Wise Men

Many years ago, under a vast, velvety sky, a single star blazed brighter than any the three wise men had ever seen. Melchior, Caspar, and Balthazar were no ordinary men; they were scholars who studied the stars, like others studied books. This star, though, pulsed with a strange energy, a message waiting to be read.

One cold night, as they huddled around their flickering campfire, a radiant figure descended from the heavens. The wise men gasped, not in fear, but in awe. The angel's voice, though powerful, was gentle. "Do not be afraid," it was heard. "This star is here to announce the arrival of a most special child, a king unlike any other."

Excitement crackled in the air. A new king? This was a journey they couldn't refuse. They packed their camels with treasures fit for royalty – gleaming gold, fragrant incense used in temples, and precious myrrh, an oil used for important blessings. With the star as their guiding light, they embarked on a long and difficult trek.

Over scorching deserts and rugged mountains they journeyed, their eyes never leaving the bright, beacon light above. Finally, after months of travel, the star dipped low, hovering over a humble stable in Bethlehem. A hush fell over the wise men as they approached. Inside, bathed in a soft glow, lay a baby boy nestled in a manger.

Reverently, the wise men kneeled. This was not an ordinary child. Melchior presented his gift of gold, a symbol of the king's nobility. Caspar offered the sweet-smelling incense, a sign of the baby's divine presence. Balthazar, with a tear in his eye, gave his myrrh, a symbol of the hardships the child might face in his life.

Mary and Joseph, filled with wonder, listened as the wise men recounted their incredible journey, led by the celestial star. The time came for the wise men to depart. But in a dream that night, an angel appeared with a warning. King Herod, a powerful yet cruel ruler, intended to harm the baby. Following the angel's message, the wise men chose a different path home, carrying a piece of the magic they had witnessed in the stable. They knew, deep down, that baby Jesus was destined for greatness, and their encounter with the newborn king, changed them forever.

True wisdom lies in seeking and recognizing the importance of love and humility, not wealth.

Asher's Journey

Asher the sparrow woke up with a chirp and a mission, a question buzzing in his tiny head. He had overheard whispers carried on the breeze - whispers about a special baby born in Bethlehem. A baby unlike any other, some said, maybe even a king! Intrigued, Asher ruffled his feathers and decided he simply had to see for himself. He tucked a plump, juicy worm he had saved from breakfast into a hidden nook of his feathers, and with a determined chirp, Asher darted off towards Bethlehem.

He wasn't the only one on the lookout, though. A sleek cat named Milly, lounging on a fence, spotted Asher. "Hey, birdie, where are you going in such a hurry?" she purred, stretching out a paw. "Off to see the baby king!" chirped Asher, flying a little faster. Milly's eyes gleamed. "Hold on a sec," she whispered playfully, batting her eyelashes. "I have the perfect gift! The most beautiful ball of yarn!" Asher, remembering all the bedtime stories his mom used to tell him about cats, shook his head and kept flying.

Next, a huge shadow fell over Asher. It was Max the eagle, circling like a feathered fighter jet. "Where to, little dude?" he asked. "Visiting the baby king!" Asher chirped, barely dodging a giant claw. Max swooped close; a feather tucked in his beak. "Here, take this magnificent feather!" Asher, remembering how eagles liked to "take on a ride" baby bunnies sometimes, politely declined and flew on.

Next, appeared Rey the fox, notorious for his sneaky tricks. "What's up, birdie?" he said. "I am going to meet the baby king!" chirped Asher, perching on a high branch to get some rest - out of pounce-range of course. Rey held up a shiny pebble. "A dazzling gift for the king!" Remembering all the missing chickens Rey "borrowed" from the farm, Asher thanked him but refused and just kept flying.

Day and night he traveled, guided by the brightest star he had ever seen. Finally, in a cozy stable, Asher found Mary, Joseph, and a tiny baby. It was the king! Asher landed on a beam; his heart full of joy. He chirped his sweetest song, a melody of happiness. Mary and Joseph smiled, and the baby king cooed in his sleep. Asher puffed his chest; happy he had made it. He might not have had a fancy gift, but his journey, filled with smarts and bravery, led him to the greatest gift of all – seeing the baby king with his own little eyes!

Trust your instincts and stay true to your path, especially when faced with deceit.

A Call to Santa

Christmas was approaching, and Evelyn's friends were chattering like excited squirrels. They were busy writing long letters to Santa, filled with wishes for all sorts of big, flashy toys. Mina wanted a bike with red wheels, Jack begged for a train set that could chug through the living room, and Lucy dreamed of a dollhouse with furniture so tiny like pebbles.

But Evelyn had a big problem. Unlike her friends, she hadn't learned how to write yet. All those squiggly lines looked like spaghetti to her! Determined to reach Santa, Evelyn hatched a daring plan – a phone call! Grabbing the phone, she dialed a bunch of numbers, listening carefully after each "beep." One sounded like an angry grandpa, another like a giggling baby.

None of them sounded like Santa! Finally, after what felt like forever, a loud voice filled the receiver. "Ho ho ho! Merry Christmas!" it said. This had to be Santa! "Santa, it's Evelyn!" she squeaked, barely containing her excitement. "I can't write yet, so I called to tell you what I want for Christmas!" A warm, friendly chuckle came through the phone. "Well, hello, Evelyn! That's a very special way to get in touch. What's on your Christmas wish list, my dear?"

Evelyn took a deep breath. "I have this beautiful doll named Rosie," she explained. "She's my best friend, but she's getting a little, well, raggedy. You see, just like me, she's all grown up now. I don't sleep with Mommy and Daddy anymore, and I think Rosie shouldn't sleep with me either. She needs her own grown-up bed!" Santa let out a jolly ho-ho-ho. "That's the most thoughtful thing I've heard all year, Evelyn! A doll bed for Rosie sounds perfect. I'll make sure the elves use their tippy-toes and quietest hammers to build it, so it's extra comfy for your best friend." "Thank you, Santa! I know Rosie will love it! Merry Christmas!" said Evelyn, filled with joy. "Merry Christmas, Evelyn," replied Santa. "You seem to understand that the best presents for Christmas aren't always wrapped in shiny paper. It's the love and joy we share with our friends, even the raggedy ones, that makes the day truly magical!"

After hanging up, Evelyn couldn't stop smiling. The wait for Christmas morning felt like forever, but finally, the big day arrived! She raced downstairs, and there, under the twinkling lights of the tree, sat a beautifully wrapped present with her name on it. Evelyn tore open the paper and gasped. Inside was the most perfect doll bed she had ever seen, just the right size for Rosie. It had a fluffy mattress, a tiny patchwork pillow, and a cozy blanket with little embroidered stars. It was like something out of a fairy tale! Evelyn gently tucked Rosie into her new bed. "See, Rosie?" she whispered. "You have your grown-up bed now, just like me. Santa listened! Merry Christmas, my best friend!"

Growing up means learning to be independent and finding ways to do things on your own.

Earthly Mission

Celeste, Gabriel, and Seraphina weren't your typical angels. Sure, they had fluffy white wings and halos that blinked on and off, but these little angels were bored! Every day was white clouds and harp practice. Yawn. One day, peeking through a cloud hole, they spotted Earth. Unlike their peaceful home, it was a jumble of honking cars, crying babies, and angry-looking grown-ups. "Hey," said Celeste, the one with a halo that kept flickering, "Earth looks like it needs a serious case of the giggles!"

So, they buzzed down to their Big Angel, who looked like a big marshmallow with even bigger wings. "Big Angel," piped up Gabriel, the angel with a voice that squeaked like a recorder, "can we go down and cheer everyone up?" The Big Angel chuckled, a sound like loud thunder. "Off you go, little ones. Remember, even silly things can make a big difference!"

First stop, Busytown! Here, they found Mr. Moody-Gills, who had burnt his toast and lost his keys. Celeste, ever the charmer, gave him the biggest, toothiest grin, and wouldn't you know it, a friendly neighbor came by with a spare key and a plate of delicious pancakes! Mr. Moody-Gills ended up having the best breakfast ever (and maybe even a giggle).

Next, they were off to a dusty village. The well was dry, and poor Molly, a little girl with long pigtails, looked about to cry. That's when Gabriel did his best rain dance, complete with goofy spins and wiggles. Suddenly, a geyser of water whooshed out, soaking everyone (including Gabriel) - but hey, at least they had water to splash in!

Their last stop was a crowded camp. A lonely boy named Ahmed sat huddled in a corner. Seraphina plopped down beside him and started juggling glowing bubbles. Ahmed, forgetting his worries, chased the bubbles giggling. Soon, everyone was joining in the bubbly fun, and the camp, for a moment, wasn't so sad anymore. With their hearts full of happy memories, the little angels flew back to the Big Angel. "You did brilliantly!" he said, filled with pride. "Remember, a little kindness can go a long way!" The three angels, blinking happily, knew they would never be bored again. After all, Earth was full of people who could truly use the help of an angel!

Small acts of kindness and compassion can bring hope and healing to those in need.

The Christmas Doll

Big City was a dazzling blur of Christmas lights and carols, loud enough to wake a hibernating bear. Outside the biggest toy store, Sonia sniffled, nose pressed against the glass. There, behind a mountain of fluffy reindeer, sat the most incredible doll ever! Gigantic, bright blue eyes and a dress redder than a fire truck – it was perfect! But with a sigh, Sonia shuffled her feet. That doll cost more than her entire piggy bank savings, and Santa probably wouldn't bring a present that big anyway. Besides, where would he even put it in his sleigh?

Meanwhile, inside the store, Mary sashayed through the aisles with her grandma, who loved to spoil her by buying her expensive gifts. Mary had her eye on the same mega-doll, and Grandma, ever the treat dispenser, happily added it to their basket. "And to make it even more magical," Grandma winked, picking out a sparkly book filled with fantastical stories, "here's a book full of fairy tale adventures!" Leaving the store, Mary clutched the big doll like a long-lost friend. Just then, Sonia, with her big eyes even bigger, stood before them. "Wow!" she exclaimed, "Isn't that the most amazing doll ever?!"

Mary peeked into Sonia's sparkly eyes and felt a sting in her heart. Glancing at her grandma, who gave a thumbs-up, Mary knew what she had to do. With a big smile, Mary came closer and placed the doll in Sonia's arms. Sonia's jaw dropped. "For real? Are you sure?" she squeaked, her voice wobbly with excitement. Mary nodded. "Absolutely! I think this doll will have way more fun playing with you! You seem to love her more than me." Sonia squeezed the doll as tight as she could. "Thank you! Thank you, a million times!" she said, then dashed off to show her family her incredible new friend.

Mary watched her go, a warm feeling spreading through her tummy. Grandma patted her hand and placed the fairy tale book in her arms. "You're a kind soul, Mary," she said, her voice soft like falling snow. "And guess what? This book is all yours for being so awesome!" Mary hugged the book to her chest, a smile stretching across her face. Maybe she didn't have the big doll, but as she snuggled into bed with her new book, she knew the true magic of Christmas wasn't about getting the biggest gift, but about the warm, fuzzy feeling that came from sharing kindness with others. After all, a happy heart was the best Christmas present anyone could ask for!

The true spirit of Christmas is about giving and sharing joy with others, not just receiving gifts.

A Meeting at the Gate

The wind howled like a wolf on the last night of December. Down the street shuffled a very old man. It was Old Year, his hair as white as fresh fallen snow and his steps a bit shaky. But even with his slow walk, his eyes seemed content, as if they had seen all they needed to see. He wore a long, dark coat that flapped in the wind. Yep, Old Year was wrapping up his time and getting ready to pass the torch. Up ahead, a big, glittery gate glowed in the distance. Behind it, clouds and smiling angels with feathery wings waited to welcome him.

As he approached, he spotted a young, energetic boy walking down the path. This was New Year, barely out of his teens and bursting with excitement. "Hey there, young one!" said Old Year with a smile. "I have been waiting for you!" New Year grinned back. "Hello! Time for me to take over and start this year rolling!" Old Year nodded, his eyes twinkling with memories. "Oh, I have stories for you," he said. "A big bag full of them! From happy tears to sniffles, belly laughs to hiccups, brand-new beginnings, and goodbyes that made hearts squeeze. I made a bunch of memories for everyone." New Year leaned in, all ears. Old Year filled him in on amazing things – people falling in love, tiny babies arriving, dreams taking flight, and tough problems being tackled. He told stories of kindness that made hearts glow, friendships that grew stronger, and people bouncing back from tricky times.

"These memories are my treasures," Old Year said gently. "They show how amazing and strong people can be." New Year, touched, put a hand on Old Year's shoulder. "Don't worry, I'll keep them safe," he promised. "I'll tuck them away in everyone's hearts, and make sure they remember all the good stuff. Plus, I'll add a million new memories – filled with laughter, fun, and exciting adventures!"

Old Year felt a big whoosh of relief. "Thank you, kiddo," he sighed happily. "Knowing my memories are in good hands makes this goodbye a breeze." With a last hug, Old Year walked through the glittery gate. New Year waved goodbye, then turned to face the world ahead. His heart thumped with excitement; his mind buzzed with ideas. It was time to start his own journey, filling the days with brand-new stories and unforgettable moments. As the clock struck midnight, fireworks lit up the sky. No one knew about the special changing of the guard, but one thing was for sure – the year ahead was a blank page, waiting to be filled with amazing memories!

Each year carries its own unique memories and lessons; with every new year come new experiences.

New Year's Resolution

Bobby the panda was the king of naps. Breakfast? Maybe later. Playtime? Eventually! School? Well, let's just say the morning announcements were usually over by the time Bobby lumbered in. One New Year's Eve, Bobby sat with his family by the fire. His dad promised to trade bamboo for yummy salads (yuck), and Mom vowed to bake a new cake every month. Now that was a resolution Bobby could get behind! When it was Bobby's turn, he scratched his head. "I want to be... early... bird?" he mumbled, then perked up. "No, even better! I'll be On-Time Panda!" His family cheered, uncertain at first about how he would achieve that. But Bobby was determined. No more missing out on fun in the bamboo forest because of sleep!

The next day, Operation Early Bird began. Bobby placed his alarm clock next to his bed, set enough alarms to wake the whole forest, and even laid out his clothes for the next day. But when the first alarm screeched, Bobby sleepily swatted it into snooze mode. The second and third alarms met the same fate. Finally, Bobby got up, fur standing on end. "Noooo! Super mega late!" He scrambled out of bed, somehow managing to put on his uniform with the shirt tucked into his pants, and then tripped over his own foot on the way out the door. School was a blur of giggles. "Looking sharp, Bobby!" Moira, his panda friend, teased him, showing him, he had his uniform backward. Bobby blushed but even he had to giggle. "New Year, new me, right? Still working on the early part..."

Determined to do better, Bobby went full-on ninja mode the next day. His alarm clock was banished across the room, and his little brother, Bo, was bribed with extra bamboo shoots to become his personal wake-up call, by jumping on him! The alarm blared, and Bobby rolled across the room to shut it off. Just as he was about to return to dreamland, a small panda landed on him with a thud! "Up and at them, sleepyhead!" Bo yelled. Bobby, wide awake now (and a little bruised), got dressed and raced to school, arriving just as the bell rang.

Mr. Hoot, their owl teacher, raised an eyebrow. "Nearly there, Bobby! Keep it up!" The following weeks were a hilarious mix of chaos and tiny triumphs. There were snoozed alarms, tangled shoelaces, and a memorable incident involving mismatched socks and a very confused-looking Bobby. But slowly, surely, Bobby was getting there. His friends cheered him on, and Mr. Hoot rewarded his effort. By the end of the month, Bobby wasn't just on time, he was sometimes even early! Being On-Time Panda might have been harder than he thought, but with a little determination, Bobby proved that even the sleepiest panda could achieve his goals!

Setting goals and working towards them, can lead to improvement and success.

Santa Finds His Way

Disaster struck Simon's village. A big avalanche, like a snow monster, roared down the mountain, burying houses. Everything was gone – their cozy home, their toys, and worst of all, they couldn't find their fluffy cat, Bailey. Christmas wasn't exactly merry that year. Simon's family huddled in a crowded camp with other families who had also lost their homes. The days were cold, and the nights seemed to last forever. While they were sharing tents and campfire stories, Simon couldn't shake the worry about Bailey. What if his cat was all alone in the snow? Or maybe she found a new home?

Christmas came and went, with no presents under the tree. Then, New Year's arrived, and still no Santa. Simon felt horrible. Like losing Bailey and the mountain being angry at them, weren't enough... Now Santa had also forgotten about him. One day, the grown-ups decided to chase away the blues with a camp dance party! They dragged out a big Christmas tree and decorated it with lights, even though the holiday was long gone. Music filled the air, and people started stomping their feet in the snow, giggling like a bunch of penguins on ice skates.

Simon, however, sat by the fire, chin resting on his knees. His dad scooped him up and twirled him around. "Hey there, Gloomy Gus!" he said. "Look under the Christmas tree!" Simon trudged over, his boots squelching in the snow. There, nestled beneath the sparkly lights, sat a box with a tag that read "Simon." A flicker of hope sparked in his eyes. But then he mumbled, "It's probably for someone else. Santa doesn't even know I'm here!" His mom, with a smile, nudged him gently. "Maybe it is for you! Go on, peek inside." Taking a deep breath, Simon opened the box. Curled up inside, a little cold but looking perfectly happy, was a tiny ball of fur, a small cat. "Who's your new friend?" his dad asked, with a wide grin.

Tears welled up in Simon's eyes, but this time they were happy tears. "Her name is Bailey," he said, holding the kitten close. "She looks just like my old Bailey!" That night, snuggled up in his sleeping bag with his new Bailey purring next to him, Simon felt a warmth spreading through him, chasing away the cold and the worry. He had his family, a new furry friend, and a heart full of hope. Maybe Christmas magic could find you anywhere, even in a snowy camp! The next day, the entire camp buzzed with the story of Simon's Christmas cat. Even though they had lost so much, hope had found a way back into their hearts.

No matter how lost you feel, hope and joy can find you when you least expect it.

Lion Adopts Boy

Rowan the lion was on his morning walk, stretching his paws and sniffing the air, when a tiny cry squeaked through the trees. Rowan followed the sound and found a baby boy nestled in a grassy patch, looking up with wide, curious eyes. "Well, hello there, little fella," Rowan rumbled gently, nudging the baby with his nose. The baby giggled and grabbed a fistful of Rowan's mane. "Hmm, you need a name," Rowan thought, stroking his chin. "I think I'll call you Hector!"

But Rowan wasn't sure how to raise a human baby. Lions mostly ate zebra burgers, not exactly baby food. So, he trotted over to Elliot the elephant, the jungle's wisest inhabitant. "Elliot, I found a human baby and I want to adopt him," Rowan explained, holding Hector carefully in his big paws. Elliot's trunk shot up in surprise. "A lion raising a human? That's crazier than a monkey wearing a tutu!" However, seeing the determined look in Rowan's eyes, Elliot finally said, "Alright then! Since humans adopt animals, I don't see why an animal cannot adopt a boy. Hector is your cub, officially!"

Hector's life in the jungle was a wild adventure! First, there was the food situation. Rowan offered Hector a zebra steak, but the baby scrunched up his nose. "Nope, not on the menu, I guess!" Rowan realized humans liked different things – juicy berries and yellow bananas became Hector's favorites. Soon, Rowan was the best berry finder in the whole jungle!

Next came roar practice. Rowan let out a mighty roar that shook the leaves. Hector puffed up his chest and tried to copy him, but all that came out was a squeak that sounded like a... baby. Bath time was equally hilarious. Rowan loved splashing in the river, but Hector preferred a mud puddle. Rowan tried to nudge him into the deeper water, but Hector just splashed and giggled. In the end, Rowan let Hector play in the mud – that's how he liked his bath after all!

Despite the funny situations, Rowan and Hector became best buds. Rowan taught Hector to be brave, while Hector filled Rowan's days with laughter. The other animals watched amazed as Hector grew up, swinging through trees like a monkey and knowing the jungle like the back of his hand. Years flew by, and Hector became a strong young man. One afternoon, as they sat on a hill overlooking the jungle, Hector looked at Rowan. "Thanks for everything! You're the best dad a kid could ask for." Rowan purred "And you are the best son a lion could ask for. We're a family, and that's the coolest thing ever in the whole jungle!"

Family is about love, care and mutual understanding, no matter how unusual it may seem.

Dream or Reality

Cecilia had a lot of fun playing with dolls, building towers that reached the ceiling, and sipping pretend tea from tiny cups, at Megan's house. But when it was time to leave, a very important someone got left behind. Mr. Snuggles, Cecilia's favorite teddy bear, was forgotten on Megan's bed! That night, climbing into bed without Mr. Snuggles felt like climbing Mount Everest in pajamas! A big frown formed on Cecilia's face. "How will I sleep without my fuzzy friend?" she wondered.

Just then, her mom peeked in with a warm smile. "Uh oh, looks like someone forgot their snuggle monster," Mom said, noticing her frowny face. Cecilia sniffled. "I left Mr. Snuggles at Megan's house! All by himself in that big bed." Mom scooped Cecilia into a hug. "Don't worry, sweetie. Mr. Snuggles is a brave bear. I bet he's having his tea party with Megan's toys. But I promise, we'll get him back tomorrow, safe and sound."

That night, Cecilia dreamed the most amazing dream. Mr. Snuggles, somehow alive (because dreams are weird and wonderful), hopped off the bed, tiptoed around Megan's house, and squeezed through a creaky door. He crossed the street, dodging big lollipop-trees and gummy worm puddles (because dream streets are crazy), and reached Cecilia's house. He climbed up the stairs, one big step at a time, and finally found Cecilia's room. With a triumphant squeak, he snuggled right next to her. In her sleep, Cecilia sighed happily, feeling the familiar sense of her best friend.

The next morning, Cecilia woke up with a smile that could light up the whole room. There, nestled beside her, was Mr. Snuggles! She squeezed him tight. "You're back! You had a crazy adventure, didn't you?" At breakfast, Mom wiggled her eyebrows. "Did you sleep well, honey?" Cecilia practically bounced in her seat.

"Yes! Mr. Snuggles came back all by himself in my dream – he even crossed the street and climbed the stairs!" Mom chuckled. "Actually, honey, Megan's parents brought him over last night. But hey, if you dream it hard enough, sometimes it feels real!" Cecilia hugged Mr. Snuggles tight. "I'm so glad you're back, my snuggly dream hero! And next time, we're holding paws out the door!" From that day on, Cecilia never left without double-checking for Mr. Snuggles. She also learned that even though dreams can be silly, sometimes they remind you how much you love something, and that feeling can be pretty magical.

When you really want something, dreams and reality can blend to make it true.

A New Tradition

The Thomas family was feeling a little blue. Christmas was over, and their living room looked bare without the sparkly Christmas tree. Danielle and Susan, the tiniest Thomases, huddled together with sad frowns. "I miss the twinkly lights," Susan sniffled. Danielle poked a droopy ornament. "Yeah, and the funny singing Santas that got stuck playing over and over." Their mom kneeled and gave them both a hug. "I know you don't like saying goodbye to Christmas, but guess what? We can still make this day a little less gloomy!" Danielle and Susan's sad faces perked up. "Awesome! How?" they asked in unison.

Their dad, the king of fun ideas, grinned. "What if, instead of just feeling sad, we plant our own tiny Christmas trees? Trees that we can watch grow all year long!" The girls' eyes widened. "Grow our own Christmas trees? Like magic?" Dad chuckled. "Not exactly magic, but pretty cool too! We can pick out special seeds and watch them sprout into little baby trees. Then, next Christmas, we can decorate them ourselves – the tiniest, most wonderful Christmas trees ever!" Danielle and Susan squealed with excitement. Tiny Christmas trees they could grow themselves? This was way better than leftover Christmas cookies!

So, bundled up like little explorers, the Thomas family marched to the garden center. It was a jungle of colorful flowers and funny-looking cacti. The girls giggled as they picked out seeds for all sorts of trees – tall and skinny ones, short and bushy ones, and even a few with pretty, purple flowers. Back home, they became official tree planters. Each girl got a small pot and some soil, and they carefully planted the seeds. They giggled as they patted the soil and pretended to whisper growing spells to their tiny seeds.

Dad showed them how to place the pots by the sunniest window and water them. Days turned into weeks, and the girls kept checking on their pots every morning. Then, one day, tiny green shoots popped out of the soil! Danielle and Susan danced around the small pots – their baby Christmas trees were coming to life! They decorated their pots with stickers and named each little tree with funny names. As the months flew by, their tiny trees grew bigger and stronger.

Finally, Christmas arrived again! The Thomases decorated their big Christmas tree, but this year, there was something extra special. They proudly placed their little trees next to it, all decorated with tiny twinkling lights. The living room glowed with festive cheer. Danielle and Susan grinned at their mini masterpieces. "These are the best Christmas trees ever!" Danielle declared. This new Christmas tradition wasn't just about growing trees, it was about growing memories, togetherness, and the magic of watching something small become something special.

Cherish what you have but look forward to the future; special things that you don't have year-round.

The Missing Rain Boots

Rain splattered on Donna the duck's window like tiny, drumming frogs. It was market day, and Donna needed juicy vegetables for her yummy duck salad. But there was a problem. A big, floppy problem. "Quack! Quack!" Donna waddled around her house like a detective searching for clues. "Where in the world did I put my rain boots?" She looked under the rug where she sometimes hid spare crackers (just in case), behind the flowery curtains (because who knew, maybe the boots liked the view), and even peeked in the fridge (hey, a duck can dream). But her bright yellow rain boots were nowhere to be found.

Then she started asking around. First stop: Mrs. Hoot, the owl who lived next door. "Mrs. Hoot," Donna quacked, "have you seen my rain boots? The market awaits, and my poor feet are begging for protection from the puddly streets!" Mrs. Hoot hooted thoughtfully. "Hmm, I haven't seen them, Donna. But have you checked the usual hiding spots for lost ducky things?" Donna sighed. "Everywhere! Under the flowerpot, behind the birdbath, even in the laundry basket with yesterday's muddy socks, although, that would be weird, even for me!"

Next, Donna hopped over to Mr. Hopper's burrow. "Mr. Hopper," she asked, "by any chance have you seen my wellies?" (Mr. Hopper was English.) "My salad is missing some crunchy goodness!" Mr. Hopper twitched his nose. "Hmm, let me think... no, no sign of them popping by this burrow." Donna waddled back home, quacking in frustration.

She retraced her steps, picturing where she might have left them. But her memory was as foggy as the rainy weather. Just as she decided to brave the puddles barefoot, something strange happened. A soft "thunk" echoed in the room as Donna opened her green umbrella. Something had fallen from above! Looking down, she saw... her bright yellow rain boots! Donna burst out laughing.

"Oh, quackers! There you are! I guess I should have hung you properly, instead of using you as a fancy hat stand!" With her rain boots secured, and her umbrella held high, Donna waddled to the market, splashing happily through the puddles. The rain didn't bother her anymore, and she even sang a silly song about forgetful ducks and upside-down rain boots. At the market, she picked out her vegetables and, as a reward for her adventure, got an extra-delicious cookie. As she waddled home, belly full and heart happy, Donna knew one thing for sure: from now on, her rain boots would always have a proper home, far away from any umbrella stands!

Keeping things in their proper place helps us find them easily when we need them.

The Magical Statue

Prince Michael of Elwood was tired of princess parades. Every day, it seemed like another princess arrived at the castle, all with sparkles, tiaras, and enough perfume to knock out a dragon. But none of them made Prince Michael feel... happy inside. "Mom," he declared to Queen Eleanor, who was busy juggling paperwork and a rather moody unicorn that kept trying to rewrite the tax laws with its horn. "I'm getting married, but I don't want a princess bride." The queen choked on her royal tea. "No princesses? But Michael, it's tradition! Besides, who else is going to wear all these extra tiaras we keep getting?"

Prince Michael, however, had a plan. "I want someone kind, someone with a heart as shiny as a new knight's armor! We'll have a test!" So, the prince invited every princess in the land. They came with fluffy poodles, mountains of cotton candy (because, really, who travels without cotton candy), and even a princess who rode a unicycle (though that ended poorly for a nearby flowerpot). One by one, the princesses paraded past a funny-looking statue in the grand hall.

Now, this wasn't your ordinary statue – it had a special talent for snorting and wiggling its eyebrows at anyone who wasn't exactly honest or kind. Unfortunately, for the princesses, the statue did a lot of eyebrow wiggling. Prince Michael was starting to think true kindness was rarer than a friendly dragon.

Just then, a quiet girl named Sophia walked in front of the statue. She wasn't a princess, but she was carrying a tray of cookies for everyone. The statue, for the first time all day, stood perfectly still. No eyebrow wiggling, no snorting! "Aha!" Prince Michael exclaimed, with a smile finally on his face. "Who is that?" "That's Sophia, Princess Amelia's servant," explained his advisor. Intrigued, Prince Michael talked to Sophia. She wasn't sophisticated or perfume-y, but she loved helping others.

She even had a dream of building a big playground for all the children in the kingdom. Although her clothes were plain, her eyes held a warmth that shone brighter than any jewel. Prince Michael knew he had found his perfect match – a kind heart shines brighter than any tiara! The queen, well, the queen eventually got used to the idea, especially after Sophia promised to wear all the tiaras! And so, Prince Michael and Princess Sophia ruled Elwood, proving that kindness is the most important quality of all!

Money and titles are less important than character and heart; that's the true worth.

The Canning Wildcat

Once upon a time, a mischievous wildcat named Kirk lived in the forest near a farm. Now, Kirk wasn't your average mouser. He had a soft spot for, well, let's just say canned tuna wasn't his only craving. Those plump, clucking chickens on the Jones farm were his ultimate temptation! One morning, Kirk overheard the farmer talking about the chickens being sick. His ears twitched – this was his chance! "Aha!" he thought, a sly grin spreading across his whiskered face. "I'll disguise myself as a doctor and snatch a few chickens for lunch!"

Kirk rummaged through some old camping gear and found a tattered white coat and a funny-looking ear trumpet. Feeling like a super sneaky vet, he practiced his most important-sounding voice and marched towards the farm. "Greetings, feathered friends!" he announced, hanging by the fence outside the coop. "I'm Dr. Kirk, here to cure your woes!"

The chickens, though a little weak, weren't fooled for a second. They had heard the rumors about Kirk's love for chicken stew. Henny, the wisest and the nosiest hen, clucked to the others. In a flash, they hatched a plan. "Oh, Dr. Kirk," Henny said, pretending to be weak, "we're so glad you're here! But there's a special cure for our sickness. We need the freshest stream water, delivered every day. We can't get better if you come too close, though!"

Kirk's ears perked up. Fresh water sounded easy enough, and he could still wait for the perfect moment to grab a drumstick. "Fresh water, you say? Anything for my precious patients!" The next day, Kirk trotted back with a bucket of water, feeling rather pleased with himself. "How are my feathery friends feeling today?" he called out from a safe distance. "A little better, Dr. Kirk," Henny clucked back. "But more water would be delightful!"

This silly dance continued for a whole week. Kirk delivered water daily, hoping his feathered friends would let their guard down. But the chickens were getting stronger by the day. They saw through Kirk's plan and kept him far away with their clever trick.

Finally, after two weeks of water duty, Kirk lost his patience. "Alright, alright! When can I come in and check on you all?" he grumbled. Henny hooted with laughter. "Dr. Kirk, you've been a big help (sort of), but the truth is, fresh air and rest are all we really needed. Thank you for the water delivery, but from now on, stay away!" Kirk realized he had been outsmarted by a bunch of chickens! Feeling defeated and quite grumpy, he slunk back to the forest. Canned tuna suddenly seemed a lot more appealing. After all, who needs feathers when you have perfectly good tins of fish?

Helping others is good, but only if your intentions are sincere.

A Winter Lesson

One snowy morning, a deceiving sun peeked through the clouds, pretending it was summer. Mommy Bunny, ever the optimist, saw its sunshine and declared, "Bundle up, little buns! We're going on an adventure!" The little bunnies, Pip, Pop, and the tiniest one, Gray, scurried around, pulling on their warmest hats and coats. But Gray, a stubborn little fellow, refused to put on his coat and scarf. "Nope! No scarf for me! I'm not cold, and this sunshine practically screams 'beach day!'" Mommy Bunny kneeled, her nose twitching. "Sunshine might be fooling around, Gray, but winter's still here. Trust me, a scarf is your friend today."

Gray puffed out his chest. "I don't need a scarf! I'm tough like a... well, like a tiny, fluffy bunny!" With a sigh, Mommy Bunny decided not to fight it. She bundled up the other bunnies and hopped out the burrow, leaving Gray with a defiant wiggle of his nose. At first, Gray felt like a champion. The sun tickled his fur, and he skipped through the snow, leaving a trail of tiny paw prints. But as they ventured deeper into the forest, the air turned chilly. Gray shivered, but pretended it was just a playful breeze.

They chased snowflakes, built a mini-snowman (well, more like a snow-bunny), and played hide-and-seek behind snowy bushes. But with every giggle and hop, Gray felt the cold creeping in. His nose turned pinker than a strawberry, and his paws felt like popsicles. He peeked at his cozy siblings, all bundled up and warm, and a tiny voice inside him whispered, "Maybe the scarf wasn't such a bad idea after all..." Mommy Bunny, with her bunny-mama superpower of noticing everything, saw Gray shivering. She picked him up and hugged him. "Feeling a bit chilly now, little explorer?"

Gray sniffled, a tear rolling down his whiskers. "Yes, Mommy! I'm soooo cold. I should have listened." Mommy Bunny smiled. "We all make mistakes, sweetie. But the best part is learning from them!" She pulled out the colorful scarf, wrapped it around Gray's neck, and held him close until he stopped shivering. From that day on, Gray never argued about scarves again. He learned that even the brightest sunshine can't fool winter, and a warm scarf can be the best adventure buddy a bunny could ask for!

It's important to listen to those who care about us, especially when they're trying to keep us safe.

Shop Green

With his backpack on and reusable bags in hand, Derek bounced with excitement. Today wasn't just grocery shopping with Mom, it was a mission! A super-secret, planet-saving mission: Operation Less Trash! "Remember, Derek," Mom said, peeking into a cart overflowing with plastic wrap, "we're on a quest to find the least wasteful stuff!"

Derek, who knew plastic mountains were bad for the oceans and hurt the animals, nodded seriously. "Like Mrs. Turner says, less plastic, happier planet!" Their first stop was Fruit and Vegetables Central. Derek scrunched his nose at the sad-looking apples in plastic prisons. "Ew, these need rescuing!" he declared. Mom grabbed a bunch of loose, shiny apples instead. "Much better," she winked.

Next, they reached a huge bin filled with grains and cereals. Mom whipped out a cool, cloth bag. "Time to ditch the plastic bags and fill this bad boy with yummy rice!" Derek scooped the grains with a grin. "This is like playing a treasure hunt, but for the Earth!" Derek spotted words like "eco-friendly" on some packages as they kept exploring. "Hey Mom, what does that fancy word mean?" Mom ruffled his hair. "That means the company cares about the planet! Maybe they use recycled boxes or make their products without hurting animals."

Suddenly, Derek stopped in front of a cleaning spray with a weird label. "Look, Mom, this bottle wants to be a plant when it grows up!" He pointed to a sticker that said "biodegradable." Mom explained, "Yep, that means it won't sit in a landfill forever. It will be broken down eventually. Pretty cool, right?"

Derek held the bottle with newfound respect. "Wow, shopping can be like a detective game for secret eco-warriors!" By the checkout, their cart was overflowing with treasures – loose apples, happy rice in a cloth bag, and an eco-friendly cleaning spray. Derek couldn't wait to tell his friends about their adventure. Smiling, Mom squeezed his hand. "You see, Derek, even small choices can make a big difference. We're a team, and together, we can fight the plastic villains, one shopping trip at a time!"

Choosing products with minimal packaging and supporting eco-friendly companies helps protect our planet.

Kelly's Presents

Kelly's room was a toy explosion zone! Shiny new dolls with golden hair lay forgotten next to mountains of colorful building blocks. A whole zoo of stuffed animals, from cuddly pandas to funky green alligators, sprawled everywhere. Even Sparky, the robotic dog with flashing lights and a barking voice, seemed to be hiding under a pile of clothes. In the middle of this toy avalanche, Kelly sat happily, playing with... a beat-up old teddy bear. It was missing an eye and had a permanent lopsided grin, but to Kelly, it was the best friend a kid could ask for.

"Kelly!" Mom called from the doorway. "Your room looks like a hurricane came through a toy store!" Kelly peeked over a mountain of blocks. "Oops! Sorry, Mom." Mom sat with her. "It's okay, honey, but you know, there are so many kids that don't get any presents at Christmas. Maybe some of all these toys could make another kid happy?" Kelly's smile faded. "But... these are my toys!" Mom hugged her. "I know, sweetie. But wouldn't it be cool to share the fun? Imagine a kid who gets a beautiful doll, or building blocks that can make a huge castle!" Kelly thought for a moment. Maybe sharing her toys wasn't such a bad idea after all. Especially if it meant another kid could build a huge castle!

So, Kelly and Mom started sorting. They picked out some dolls, a few blocks, and Sparky (who secretly seemed relieved to escape the toy pile). They even added the fanciest dress-up clothes and the cutest toy kitchen set. Each toy they chose brought back a memory of fun times, but now, they were also filled with the hope of making someone else smile.

The next day, they packed the toys into the car and drove to the local shelter. There, a friendly lady greeted them with a warm smile. "These toys are amazing!" she exclaimed. "The kids are going to be thrilled! Kelly, a little shy at first, handed over each toy carefully. As she imagined the joy on the kids' faces, a happy feeling bubbled up in her tummy. It felt even better than getting a new toy herself!

On the way home, Kelly looked out the window, a big grin on her face. "I'm glad we shared, Mom. Sharing feels way better than keeping everything to myself." Mom squeezed her hand. "You're absolutely right, Kelly. You made a lot of kids happy today, and that's something to be proud of!" That night, Kelly snuggled up with her trusty teddy bear. She didn't really need a room overflowing with toys. Besides, the best kind of fun comes from sharing and making others smile. And who knows, maybe someday, she'll get to play with those happy kids and build the biggest, most awesome castle ever!

Sharing something you love, can be even more enjoyable than keeping it all to yourself.

A Dog and a Boy

William thought he was a master dog-teaser. One sunny afternoon, he turned Loki, his furry best friend, into a living train! He tied a bright red toy train to Loki's tail, giggling as the little dog chased after it, tangled in a choo-choo conga line. Then, William, inspired by a picture book, decided Loki could be a packhorse. He piled tiny books on Loki's back, making the poor pup look like a miniature librarian. Finally, he added a jingling bell necklace, transforming Loki into a walking jingle machine.

Through all this, Loki whimpered and looked less than thrilled. But William, lost in his game, didn't notice. Grandpa, chilling on the porch, watched with a worried frown. "William," he said, "that's not nice. Loki isn't having any fun! He is actually suffering!" William, however, was convinced dogs loved these games. "Don't worry, Grandpa," he said. "He's just a dog!"

That night, as William drifted off to sleep, things got weird. He shrunk smaller and smaller, fur sprouted all over him, and his voice turned into a tiny yelp! He looked down – he was a puppy! Suddenly, a boy with Loki's characteristic grin stood before him. "Ready to play, William?" he said in a voice that sounded more like a bark!

Loki (now the boy) tied a train to William's tail (ouch that hurt), then piled books on his back (double ouch). The jingling bell necklace was the final straw (well, the final jingle actually). William tried to bark "Stop!" but it came out as a whimper. Loki-boy just kept playing rough, completely ignoring William's pleas. William felt awful – tired, sore, and totally frustrated. This was exactly how Loki felt when William played too rough!

Then, with a jolt, William woke up back in his bed, his human self thankfully intact. Loki, the real Loki, was curled up at his feet, fast asleep. William gently stroked Loki, a tear rolling down his cheek. "I'm so sorry, buddy," he whispered. "From now on, only gentle games for you!" The next day, William and Loki played fetch – with a soft ball, not a train! He scratched Loki's belly and showered him with treats. Grandpa watched, a broad smile on his face. Loki's tail wagged like a metronome set on happy, and William knew he was finally treating his best friend the right way!

Treat others the way you want to be treated, whether they are people or pets.

New Baby Brother

Julia bounced with excitement – today was her baby brother's homecoming day! For weeks, she had pictured them as best buddies, sharing toys and giggling together. Maybe they would even build a blanket fort together! As dinnertime drew near, Julia could barely contain herself. "Extra plate for the baby?" she chirped to Grandma, who was busy setting the table. Grandma chuckled. "Not quite, sweetie. Babies are tiny milk-drinking machines for now, not pizza eaters." Julia's eyes widened. "Just milk? That sounds kind of boring."

Grandma kneeled. "Babies need special care, like little flowers. They grow big and strong on milk, then someday they'll join us for pizza parties!" Julia, though a little confused, grabbed her favorite stuffed animal, Mr. Fuzzy the teddy bear. He was super soft and cuddly, and Julia hoped the baby would love him too.

Finally, the front door creaked open. Julia's parents walked in, carrying a mysterious, blue-blanketed bundle. Her heart felt like it was beating faster as she tiptoed closer. "Wow, he's like a tiny, sleeping prince!" Julia whispered, peering at the little face. He was even smaller than she imagined! Mommy smiled and gently placed the prince (or maybe the tiny astronaut) in a crib. Julia stood on her tiptoes for a better look. "Can I play catch with him?" she asked, picturing herself and the baby throwing a ball to each other.

Mommy chuckled. "Hold on, champ. Your brother's very little and needs gentle care at the moment. But you can be a super big sis and help in other ways!" A tiny frown tugged at Julia's lips, but then she straightened up. "How can I help?" Mommy handed her a soft, fluffy blanket. "You can sing lullabies to him or be his blanket-bringer-in-chief! He'll love hearing your voice and feeling your love."

Julia's frown flipped upside down. "Singing and blanketing? I can definitely do that!" For days, Julia took her job very seriously. She sang silly songs (babies liked silly, right?), tucked the tiny prince in his blanket, and even made sure Mr. Fuzzy was always nearby. She even helped with diaper changes (mostly by handing over wipes and giggling at the funny smells). Every gurgle, every wiggle of tiny fingers filled Julia with a warm glow. Being a big sister wasn't just about games, it was about love, care, and maybe even a few silly songs!

Caring for a young sibling means being patient and gentle, especially when they are small.

The Latest Trend

In the heart of the most beautiful, green forest, lived a squirrel named Cassy. Now, Cassy was not an average squirrel – she was so proud of her whiskers. Long, flowing, and so elegant, they were, in her opinion, the height of squirrel fashion. But one day, Cassy was on a daring mission to snag the biggest acorn she had ever seen. As she scrambled up a scratchy tree, her whisker snagged on a twig and... it broke clean off. Cassy froze, staring at her broken whisker in horror. How could she face the world without her perfectly symmetrical whiskers?

Despair turned to a mischievous glint in Cassy's eye. If she couldn't have perfect whiskers, then maybe none of the other squirrels should either! That way, her broken whisker wouldn't seem so bad. The next morning, Cassy gathered all the squirrels under a big tree. "Attention, everyone!" she squeaked, her voice dripping with drama. "I have earth-shattering news! A wise owl hooted a secret to me – squirrels with shorter whiskers are faster and cooler!"

The other squirrels blinked. "Faster?" asked Benny, a young squirrel who worshiped Cassy's style. "But whiskers help us balance and stuff. Are you sure this owl wasn't, you know, pulling your tail?" Cassy, ever the actress, puffed out her chest. "Sure! Trust me, short whiskers are the new 'in' thing. I have already started the trend, and let me tell you, I feel like a rocket!" Some of the younger squirrels were sold. Short whiskers did sound pretty cool.

But Gracie, the elder squirrel, wasn't convinced. She narrowed her eyes, noticing Cassy's uneven whiskers. "Cassy," she said, "did you, by any chance, have a little whisker accident and are now trying to make us all bald?" Cassy stammered, then blurted, "Of course not. I trimmed them! You should all do it too! It's the rage!" Gracie wasn't born yesterday. She whispered to the others, "Let's hold off on the whisker-chopping ceremony. We'll just watch Cassy for a few days and see how 'fantastic' she feels with her new 'short and speedy' look."

The squirrels agreed. And what they saw over the next few days was hilarious! Without her full set of whiskers, Cassy became a clumsy mess. She tumbled off branches, misjudged jumps, and landed face-first in a pile of leaves – all while the other squirrels tried (and mostly failed) to stifle their laughter. Finally, Benny couldn't hold it in any longer.

"Cassy," he squeaked, "we know the truth. You didn't trim your whiskers, you lost one and tried to trick us!" Cassy drooped her ears. "Okay, okay, you got me," she sighed. "I felt weird without a perfect whisker, and I wanted you all to be weird with me." Gracie placed a paw on Cassy's shoulder. "Hey, mistakes happen," she said. "But true friends don't care about whiskers. We're here for you, even if you look a little... uneven." The other squirrels chattered in agreement. Cassy realized that looking cool wasn't as important as having good friends and maybe, a slightly trimmed whisker wasn't the end of the world after all.

Honesty and accepting our mistakes are better than trying to make others share in our misfortunes.

New Friends

Jarvis the piglet woke up with a wiggle in his curly tail. Today was the day he would meet his farmyard neighbors! He trotted to the kitchen, where Momma Pig was flipping pancakes that smelled delicious. "Can I go meet everyone, Mom?" Jarvis squealed, his hooves clicking with excitement. Momma Pig smiled. "Of course, little explorer! But first, let's get you looking perfect for some new friends." She scrubbed the mud off Jarvis's snout (pigs will be pigs), dressed him in his fanciest overalls (complete with a tiny red bowtie), and even curled his tail into a perfect little spring. "There you go," she said, bopping his nose. "Now you're a handsome piglet ready to make a splash!"

Jarvis bounced out the door, all excited. First stop: the funny-looking turkey in the next pen. "Hello, Mr. Tom Turkey!" Jarvis called out. The turkey blinked, surprised by the tiny pig with the bouncy tail. "Well, hello there, youngster! You must be Jarvis." Next, Jarvis popped by the goat pen. The goat, munching on hay, looked down at him. "Hey there, Mr. Goatee!" Jarvis greeted him. The goat bleated a friendly reply, spraying Jarvis with a bit of wet hay!

Jarvis continued his farmyard adventure, meeting the moo-cow in the meadow, the clucking chickens who gossiped like crazy, and even the playful dog who promised to teach him how to fetch (as if Jarvis, with his tiny legs, could ever catch anything). The cat, napping in a sunbeam, opened one eye and purred, "Welcome, little fella." Even the pigeons cooed a hello from the rooftop.

Finally, Jarvis reached the sheep pen. There, nestled among the wooly grown-ups, was a tiny lamb with the softest-looking fleece ever. Her name was Suzie, and she giggled when Jarvis introduced himself. "I would love to play," Suzie said, "but I have to ask my mommy first." The next day, the farmyard phone jingled! Jarvis grabbed it. "Hello?" "Hi, Jarvis! It's Suzie! My mommy said we can play! Want to meet by the big pear tree this afternoon?"

Jarvis squealed with delight. "Absolutely! See you there, Suzie!" Under the shade of the pear tree, Jarvis and Suzie became the best of friends. They chased butterflies, told each other funny animal jokes, and even got stuck together trying to share a giant lollipop! That night, Jarvis snuggled into his bed of hay, a happy sigh escaping his snout. He had a farmyard full of friends, a new best buddy in Suzie, and a heart full of happiness. And he knew, from that day on, that adventures were always just a barnyard hop away!

Making new friends can be easy and fun when you are kind and open to meeting others.

Up in the Tree

Iggy, the grizzly bear cub, was a climbing champion. Especially in winter, when the forest wore a sparkling coat of white, Iggy loved scaling the tallest trees. One morning, he spotted a big pine tree that scraped the clouds and thought, "Challenge accepted!" Up, up, and up he went, his claws digging into the rough bark like tiny grappling hooks.

Finally, he reached a high, wide branch and whoopsie-daisy! Right there, munching on an acorn, was Tina, a squirrel with a spectacular, bushy tail. Tina did a surprised squirrel-squeak. "Whoa there, Iggy! What brings you to my penthouse apartment?" Iggy grinned, his big furry cheeks stretching. "Hi, Tina! I'm climbing! Want to see?" Tina flicked her tail and giggled. "Nope! Climbing's kind of my thing, you know? This is, like, my home!" Then, with a blur of brown fur, she shot even higher, disappearing into the branches.

Iggy, curious (and maybe a little competitive), scrambled after her. As he climbed, he bumped into Becky, a tiny junco bird with feathers the color of night. Becky was perched on a branch, chirping a sweet song. "Hi there, little birdie," Iggy puffed, a little out of breath. "What are you doing way up here?" Becky tilted her head and chirped back, "Just taking a winter break, enjoying the view!" "But how did you get up here?" Iggy asked, tilting his head even further. Becky puffed out her tiny chest. "Flown here, of course! Watch this!" And with a burst of feathery wings, Becky soared into the clear blue sky, dipping and diving like a tiny acrobat.

Iggy watched, mesmerized. He wanted to fly too! To see the world from up there! Without thinking twice, Iggy took a deep breath, spread his arms, and leaped off the branch, just like Becky... Big mistake. Because grizzly bears, unlike birds, cannot fly. Iggy tumbled through the air, flailing his paws like crazy. He bounced off a few branches (ouch), but luckily, the snow was soft and fluffy underneath. With a surprised "oof," Iggy landed in a big pile of snow at the bottom of the tree.

He sat there for a moment, catching his breath and blinking snowflakes out of his eyes. Then, a bushy tail tickled him. It was Tina, looking down with concern. "Hey, Iggy, are you okay down there?" she squeaked. Iggy giggled, a little woozy but unharmed. "Yep, all good! Guess I'm a better climber than a... flyer." Becky swooped down and landed on a nearby branch. "That was a brave try, Iggy," she chirped. "But not everyone who goes up, has to come down the same way." Iggy grinned, shaking the snow off his fur. "You're right, Becky. I'll stick to climbing from now on." That night, curled up with his family, Iggy told them all about his adventure, and his very important discovery: some things are best left to the birds!

It's great to try new things, but it's also important to know your limits and stay safe.

Finding the Horizon

Ringo the blue jay was no ordinary bird. Sure, he loved worms and chatting with his neighbors, but he also craved adventure. One day, an itch formed in his tiny blue head. "Where does the sky meet the earth?" he wondered. "Is there, like, a big fence or something?" Without a moment's hesitation, Ringo spread his wings and took off. He soared over the forest, the world spreading under him. Below, a family of deer stopped mid-munch, staring at the blur of blue that was Ringo. "Whoa!" said a baby deer. "Did that jay just sprout a rocket?"

Suddenly, an owl hooted from a branch. "Ringo, where are you dashing off to, in such a hurry?" she said, her voice laced with amusement. Ringo puffed out his chest, nearly losing his balance. "I'm on a mission, wise owl! I'm finding the end of the sky!" The owl laughed. "The end of the sky, eh? That's a long flight, little one. Are you sure your tiny wings can handle it?" Ringo, never one to back down from a challenge, chirped, "Of course! Onwards to the edge of everything!" He flew past the forest, leaving the familiar behind.

Soon, Ringo found himself in a jungle so thick he could barely see the sky. Parrots squawked in a language he didn't understand, and a sneaky monkey swung down, grabbing his tail. "Whoa there, Mr. Speedy!" the monkey shrieked. "Going somewhere important?" "The end of the sky!" Ringo said, while the monkey was still dangling from his tail. The monkey pointed a hairy finger in the direction Ringo was already flying. "Keep going, little dude! You're on the right track!" Exhausted but determined, Ringo flew for what felt like forever.

Finally, he reached the big, blue ocean, its waves sparkling like scattered jewels. Below, a pod of orcas zipped past, whistling greetings. "Excuse me, Mrs. Orca!" Ringo called out, a little out of breath. "Is this where the sky ends?" An orca popped her head out of the water, spraying Ringo with a spout of water. "Nope! Keep swimming... er, I mean, flying! You're almost there!" Ringo flapped his wings and kept flying over the ocean until he spotted massive mountains scraping the clouds. Higher and higher he went, his tiny blue body a speck against the snowy peaks. On a mountain peak, perched like a statue, sat a majestic eagle. "Hey there, Mr. Eagle!" Ringo called, panting. "Is this where the sky, you know, meets the ground?"

The eagle looked down at Ringo with wise eyes. "Almost there, little bird. Just a bit further." With a final burst of energy, Ringo reached the highest peak. He gasped. The view was incredible! The earth stretched out below him, a beautiful mix of green, blue, and white. The sky seemed to go on forever, an enormous blue dome. But there was no fence, no wall, no "End of Sky" sign. Ringo realized then that the sky didn't actually end – it just kept going, just like his sense of adventure! He may not have found the edge of the sky, but he had discovered something much cooler: the thrill of exploration!

Pursue your dreams with determination, no matter how far you will have to go.

A Lonely Scarecrow

Stanley the scarecrow shivered in the snowy field. He was all alone, his straw arms flapping in the icy wind. "Wah!" he cried, a desperate, lonely sound spreading across the field. "Wah!" came a miserable reply from somewhere far away. Stanley blinked his big, button eyes. Who else could be out here, feeling as gloomy as he did? Determined to find this mystery moaner, Stanley took a wobbly step on his wooden legs. Squelch! He sank into the snow. "Need a hand... er, a twig?" squeaked a tiny voice.

A field mouse with whiskers twitching, peeked out from a snowdrift. "I'm going to find whoever's crying," Stanley mumbled. "Maybe we can be friends! Want to come?" The little mouse, whose name was Bobby, scurried up Stanley's leg. "We'll go together!" he said bravely. They trudged through the snow, Stanley creaking and Bobby shivering.

Soon, they spotted a magnificent elk with a rack of antlers like a crown. "Whoa!" Stanley cried, forgetting his mission for a moment. "Where you headed, scarecrow?" the elk asked. "Looking for the crying voice," Stanley explained. "Anyone lonely can be my friend!" The elk chuckled. "Hop on my back! We can cheer this mystery moaner up!" With Bobby tucked in his straw hat, Stanley rode the elk like a snowy chariot. They soon met a sad-looking bison plowing through the snow. "Lost, are we?" the bison snorted. Stanley explained their mission, and the bison, whose name was Bessie, decided to join the quest for the mystery moaner. They even picked up a fluffy white rabbit named Candy hopping along the way.

Finally, they reached the cliffs at the edge of the field. There, standing tall and proud, was an ancient pine tree. "Excuse me, Mr. Pine," Stanley called out. "We're looking for the friendless creature who keeps crying from this direction. We want to be their friend!" The pine tree swayed in the wind. "The moaner? He moved on," the tree said. "It was just your echo..." Stanley's straw shoulders slumped. "An echo? But I wanted a real friend."

Just then, Bobby squeaked from his hat, "But you have me, Stanley!" The elk stepped closer, "And me." The bison nodded, "Me too." The rabbit hopped up and said, "And me, too." Stanley looked around at his new crew, a smile spreading across his stitched face. He saw his new companions and realized he was no longer alone. "Right, I have many friends!" he yelled joyfully. "I have many friends," the voice replied from across the field. And so, Stanley and his new friends, a brave mouse, a goofy elk, a big bison, and a little rabbit, laughed together, their happy sounds echoing through the winter field, chasing away the cold and filling the air with friendship.

Sometimes, we don't realize how many friends we have around us, until we reach out to them.

Carter's Challenge

Carter loved chasing dodgeballs in gym class and reading stories about pirates who buried treasure. But math class? Math class was like a jungle gym made of prickly numbers and confusing equations. No matter how hard Carter climbed, he would slip and slide back down, feeling like a total failure. Every day, the math homework monster grew hungrier. Fractions turned into pizza slices with missing crusts, decimals looked like dot-to-dot puzzles gone wrong, and word problems sounded more like riddles with no answers. Carter stared at his math book until his eyes felt like they were melting. "Ugh, why can't math be about how many cookies I can eat in one sitting?" he grumbled.

One afternoon, Carter sat at the kitchen table, surrounded by a battlefield of crumpled papers and a math test that looked like a messy chicken had walked across it. His mom noticed his expression. "Hey there, Captain Crumpleface," she said. "What's got your brain in a knot?" Carter sniffled. "Math, Mom! It's like a big bully who keeps picking on me. I just don't get it!" His mom pulled him into a hug. "It's okay not to get something right away," she said. "Even superheroes need a sidekick to help them fight villains!"

But even with his mom's superhero pep talk, Carter felt like a sidekick who kept tripping over his cape. He stopped raising his hand in class, scared of getting the answer wrong. Math tests turned into report cards that read "Needs Improvement" in red letters. One day, Mrs. Thompson, his teacher, announced a pop quiz. Carter's stomach did a flip-flop, and his mind went blank. When the graded tests came back, Carter's score looked like a sad, lonely number. "Maybe I'm just not good at math," he thought, feeling defeated.

Sensing his discouragement, Mrs. Thompson kept him after class. "Carter," she said, "listen here. Math can be tricky, but you are not! Let's work together and turn those frowns upside down." Mrs. Thompson became his math coach. She broke down the problems into bite-sized pieces, used colorful charts and pictures, and even let him use counting bears.

Slowly, but surely the numbers stopped looking like they were dancing, and the equations started to click. Carter's confidence grew bigger, and he even raised his hand in class – not because he wanted to impress his teacher, but because he knew the answer! Then, one day, Mrs. Thompson handed Carter a math test. This time, he wasn't scared. He tackled the problems with a smile. When he got his test back, a happy A with a smiley face next to it, was right there staring back at him! Carter finally understood. Math wasn't a bully anymore. With a little help and a lot of determination, he had learned that even the trickiest problems can be solved.

Never give up, even when things seem difficult; face challenges and ask for help if you need it.

Reduce, Reuse, Recycle

Ugh, Saturday morning. Sunshine streaming in, birds chirping... boring! Abigail flopped dramatically on her porch swing, kicking her legs. Next door, Logan mirrored her pose, a groan escaping his lips. Suddenly, Abigail perked up. "Hey, did you hear Mrs. Turner's meltdown about trash yesterday?" Logan nodded, making a face. "Yeah, about a gazillion pounds of garbage every year! Gross!" Abigail's eyes widened. "And it all just sits in giant mountains or floats in the ocean. Disgusting!"

They both knew they had to do something, but what? Just then, a lightbulb lit up over Abigail's head. "Aha! We can raid my garage for those old boxes instead of tossing them!" Grinning like they had just won a pie-eating contest, they dashed into the garage. With a few boxes, some colorful markers the size of paintbrushes, and scissors, they got to work.

Logan, the self-appointed architect, became "Window Wizard," cutting out peepholes. Abigail, the resident artist, became "Rainbow Picasso," transforming the boxes into a masterpiece. By afternoon, their masterpiece was complete – a magnificent cardboard castle with a wiggly-wobbly drawbridge and flags made from mismatched socks. "This is the coolest fort EVER!" Logan declared, bouncing with excitement. Abigail nodded, a triumphant look in her eyes. "And guess what? We made it from stuff we already had! Reuse rocks!"

The next weekend, at Logan's house, his mom held up a mountain of empty jars and cans. "How about turning these into super cool containers for your stuff?" The kids yelled, "Recycling to the rescue!" in unison. Armed with glue, colorful paper, and stickers galore, they transformed the junk into treasures. Abigail's favorite was a jar shimmering with so much glitter it could blind them, while Logan's can sported a T-Rex sticker so fierce, it could scare away any monster under the bed. "These look amazing!" Abigail exclaimed. "And guess what? We reused things that would have gone bye-bye! Recycling superheroes, unite!"

A few days later, inspired by their creations, they decided to make recycling a family competition. The mission: find the wackiest recyclable! Abigail's dad unearthed a pile of old magazines, perfect for making funny faces. Logan's little brother, a tiny explorer, found a robot missing an arm – perfect for fighting imaginary space villains! But the winner was Abigail's mom, who presented a beautiful glass bottle shaped like a fish. They knew they were making a difference, one recycled treasure at a time. After all, saving the planet could be fun, and who knew, maybe they would even inspire grown-ups to join their recycling brigade!

Recycling helps take care of our planet, and it can be a fun and creative activity for everyone!

Making Friends

High up in a leafy eucalyptus mansion lived Wesley the koala. He was a champion leaf muncher and a top-notch climber, but lately, things felt a bit... well... lonely! One morning, while chomping on a juicy leaf, Wesley spotted a flash of gray fur in a nearby tree. "Hey there!" he yelled, waving his fuzzy paw. "I'm Wesley!" The other koala blinked and waved back. "Gooday, mate! I'm Bennett." Wesley scurried down his tree, excitement buzzing in his furry belly. "Want to play catch? I found this spiky, round thing – perfect for tossing!" Bennett's eyes lit up. "Catch? You betcha!"

They raced to a sunny clearing, the spiky ball bouncing between them. Laughter filled the air as they chased and threw, but soon, Wesley noticed something odd. Bennett clung to the ball like it was about to fly away! "Hey, Bennett," Wesley called politely. "My turn?" Bennett scrunched his nose. "Nah, mate. I'm not done yet!" Wesley's ears drooped. "But sharing is caring, remember? That way, we both get to play with the fun spiky ball." Bennett shook his head stubbornly. "Nope, mine!" Wesley sighed. Playing catch with a ball hog wasn't exactly fun. "Well," he said, "if you don't want to share, I'll just go find some other games to play."

The next day, Wesley practiced his climbing skills alone, pretending to be a koala hero. He missed having a playmate, but sharing was important, like always having extra eucalyptus leaves in case of emergencies! Bennett watched from afar, the spiky ball clutched tightly. "Hey, Wesley!" he called out. "Want to play catch again?" Wesley shook his head. "Not unless you share, Bennett. It's no fun if only one koala gets to play." Bennett scuffed his feet, feeling a bit silly. He tried playing catch by himself, but it wasn't nearly as exciting.

The day after that, Wesley was back in the clearing, building a tall leaf tower. This time, Bennett approached slowly, the spiky ball bouncing at his paw. "Wesley," he mumbled, "I'm sorry I hogged the ball. Sharing is fair, and I missed playing with you." Wesley smiled. "That's alright, mate. Sharing makes playing way more fun! Want to help me build this epic leaf skyscraper?" Bennett smiled. "You bet! And maybe we can take turns being the top koala king?" They spent the rest of the day building, tossing leaves, and taking turns being the silliest koala king anyone had ever seen. Sharing wasn't just fair, it made playing with friends much more fun!

Taking turns and sharing make playing together more fun and help build strong friendships.

Giving Love is Simple

Andrew and Ian were best friends. Stuck together like glue, they always sat next to each other in class, whispering jokes and passing notes about the latest dinosaur discoveries. But their perfect desk-mate partnership was thrown into chaos with the arrival of two new students: Borys and Albin, all the way from Poland! Mr. Anderson, their teacher, had to split Andrew and Ian up to make space for the newcomers. Andrew grumbled like a grizzly bear, and Ian sulked like a sad puppy. But Mr. Anderson, wouldn't listen.

One day, their teacher announced, "Tomorrow is Friendship Day, class! Bring a gift for your best bud!" Andrew, determined to win Ian's "Best Friend Forever" award, dug out a collection of shiny baseball cards he knew Ian would love. Ian, on the other hand, snagged a brand-new, bright orange soccer ball – perfect for Andrew's favorite sport. The next day, the classroom buzzed like a beehive! Jennifer, known for her love of baking, brought a delicious sweet potato pie that smelled like cinnamon and sunshine.

Borys, a little shy but with a warm smile, stood up holding a basket overflowing with bright red apples. "Borys," said Mr. Anderson, "want to tell us a bit about Poland?" Borys, a little nervous, sang a beautiful but slightly sad song in Polish. When he finished, the class went silent, then erupted in applause. "That song is about missing home," Borys explained, his voice soft. "I miss Poland sometimes, but I'm happy to be here and make new friends."

With that, Borys handed out apples to everyone. "Give love like you would give an apple," he said, a tiny smile playing on his lips. "As simple as that. Easy!" Andrew and Ian exchanged their gifts, both grinning like goofballs. But something strange happened. As they chomped on their yummy apples, they realized something important. Maybe Borys and Albin felt a little lonely, being new and all.

Andrew, with a mouthful of apple, looked at Borys. "Thanks for the apple, Borys," he mumbled. "And the song, that was really cool, even if it was a bit sad." Ian, still chewing on his apple, chimed in, "Yeah, thanks! Maybe you guys can join our dinosaur adventures sometime?" His smile grew even bigger. "I'd like that!" By the end of the day, the whole class was a jumble of happy chatter and shared stories. Andrew and Ian learned that friendship wasn't just about sitting next to someone, but about sharing, understanding, and welcoming new friends into their circle. After all, the more friends you have, the more adventures you can enjoy!

Friendship is about sharing, understanding, and welcoming others into your life with an open heart.

53

Maple Syrup Magic

Eric and Danny, two brothers who cared deeply for each other, lived in a town where maple trees scraped the sky. Every winter, when snow piled high, they would get an early start in their tapping business. You see, these brothers weren't just any brothers – they were maple syrup collectors! Come January, they would race through the snowy fields, the icy wind stinging their cheeks and their wooly mittens barely keeping their fingers warm. With a wink to Mr. Maple, the landowner, they would grab their toolbox and get to drilling. Tiny taps went into the trees, and soon, a magical clear liquid trickled out – sap, the future golden syrup!

Now, these brothers were the best of buds but the worst guessers, and here is why. Eric, a bachelor with a sweet tooth the size of Vermont, worried about Danny's family of four. Kids are syrup guzzlers, after all! So, each year, after their long hours of boiling sap that bubbled like a happy witch's cauldron, Eric would sneak half his jars into Danny's shed. "More syrup for the pancake people!" he would whisper to himself.

Meanwhile, Danny, with a wife who could spot a bargain a mile away, fretted about Eric's single-guy budget. "He needs that syrup money!" he would think, then secretly add half his jars to Eric's stash under the cover of night. "Extra sweetness for the solo syrup slurper!" Come spring, both Eric and Danny would be baffled. "Huh, guess we made more syrup than I remembered," they would scratch their heads, each believing they had tapped a super juicy maple tree. This silly cycle went on for years, the townsfolk raving about the brothers' endless supply of syrup.

One snowy morning, as they drilled taps with a synchronized tap-tap-tap, Eric burst out laughing. "Danny," he wheezed, "I think we have been outsmarting ourselves for years!" Danny's eyes widened, then he too roared with laughter. They spilled the beans (or should we say, the sap) about their secret stash-swapping. From that day on, their maple syrup adventures were filled with double giggles. Their syrup, sprinkled with love and brotherly goofiness, tasted even more delightful. After all, who needs a perfect plan when you have a brother who cares a sap-ton about you?

When we give from the heart, we create magic that comes back to us.

A Noisy Adventure

Beep beep! Honk honk! Mr. Decibel, a creature with a microphone head, had a taste for loud noises. He lived in a city that never stopped singing. Motorbikes roared, cars beeped like impatient birds, and jackhammers thumped on the sidewalk. Mr. Decibel loved it all! One day, a teeny-tiny beetle named Becky, fresh from the quiet forest, landed smack-dab in the middle of this noisy symphony. Her ears, usually perked for the whisper of the wind, were now overloaded! Airplanes whooshed in the sky, radios blasted like boomboxes at a bug rave, and car alarms shrieked like surprised kazoos. Becky wanted to plug her ears with flower petals!

"Whoa there, little one," a voice said. Mr. Decibel, with a handlebar mustache that twitched with every honk, approached Becky. "Looking a bit lost in the city symphony, aren't we?" "Lost and scared!" squeaked Becky. "Back in the forest, the loudest thing is a snoring ladybug! Here, it's like a million elephants and angry lions all arguing at once!" Mr. Decibel chuckled, a sound like a popcorn kernel popping. "Don't worry, little sprout. Those roaring beasts are just motorbikes, the honking things are cars with impatient drivers, and the jackhammers are, well, giant hammers for building stuff!" he added, tapping his foot rhythmically to the city sounds.

Becky blinked. "So, all this noise has a reason?" "Exactly!" replied Mr. Decibel. "The music's for dancing (or wiggling your antennae, whichever you prefer) and the airplanes take beetles on exciting vacations... well, maybe not beetles, but you get the idea!" Becky thought for a moment. "Okay, but why can't they whisper like a gentle breeze?" Mr. Decibel scratched his head with his long hand. "Hmm, good question. Maybe they just forget how nice quiet can be. But hey, even in this noisy city, we can find peaceful spots. Follow me, little sprout!" He led Becky to a secret garden hidden between buildings.

Here, the city noise became a soft hum, like a lullaby sung by a sleepy bee. Birds chirped, flowers swayed, and a gentle breeze tickled Becky's antennae. "Wow!" whispered Becky. "This is amazing! "See?" smiled Mr. Decibel. "Even in a loud world, you can always find a little quiet place. Remember, even the noisiest beetles need to rest sometimes!" From then on, Becky explored the city with newfound courage. Whenever the noise got too much, she would remember Mr. Decibel and find a quiet corner to relax. And sometimes, she would meet him in the secret garden, sharing a moment of peaceful silence, proving that even the littlest beetle can appreciate a quiet break.

Loud noises can be scary, but they have a purpose; there's always a quiet place to find peace if you look for it.

The Thirsty Rivals

Beau the boar was a snorting, snuffling mess. He had been digging for truffles all morning, and his throat felt drier than the desert! Just then, Wylie the wolf, with a tongue lolling out like a floppy red carpet, trotted up to the same stream. "Whoa, hold your bristly horses, Beau-breath!" Wylie snarled. "This water's mine! I get to have a drink first. I have been chasing rabbits for hours!" Beau snorted. "Rabbits? I chased dreams that were tastier than that! Move it, mutt!" Before you could say "mud bath," they were at it! Beau charged, hooves kicking up dirt like a furious tap dancer. Wylie dodged, snapping his teeth like a rusty zipper. They rolled in the mud, tusks clashing, fur flying, all for a sip of cool water!

Suddenly, a giant shadow loomed overhead. Vinnie the vulture, with his sharp beak and piercing gaze, circled above. "Hmm," he croaked, "looks like someone's serving a two-course meal today – boar and wolf stew!" He would wait patiently for them to finish each other off. Beau and Wylie froze. The fight drained right out of them as fast as it had started. "Uh oh," Beau whimpered, his voice cracking like a twig. "Maybe fighting for water wasn't the best idea?" Wylie gulped. "Yeah, maybe Vinnie's feast isn't on the menu today."

They both looked at each other, then at the refreshing, gurgling stream. Beau sighed. "You go first, fur-face. My turn next." Wylie dipped his head in, lapping up the water like a warm soup. Then, Beau took his turn, his snout disappearing with a happy slurp. As they drank, Vinnie grumbled something about "changing lunch plans" and soared off in search of an easier and maybe juicier target.

Beau and Wylie sat by the stream, bumps and bruises forgotten. "Well, that was silly," Beau chuckled. Wylie grinned. "Right? Maybe next time, we share the stream water. No more mud wrestling for me!" From that day on, Beau and Wylie became the unlikeliest of friends. They shared the forest's bounty, even warning each other of aggressive badgers and threatening bears. They were proof that even a boar and a wolf, with a little cooperation, could be the coolest team in the forest!

Working together, sharing and taking turns is better than fighting over things.

The Strongest Husband

In a cozy little burrow under an ancient carob tree lived a wise father mouse, named Chip, and his beautiful daughter, Trixie. As Trixie grew older, Chip knew it was time for her to start her own family. But Chip believed that Trixie was far too lovely to marry a simple mouse. She deserved someone special. But who was good enough for her? "She deserves someone strong!" Chip declared, stroking his whiskers. "Someone, well, sensational!"

Suddenly, a bright idea struck him. "The Sun! Now that's a powerful husband!" So, Chip and Trixie, with a picnic basket full of cheese, set off for the Sun's palace. The Sun, a ball of mesmerizing light, beamed down at them. "Why hello there! What brings a charming family like yours to my doorstep?" "Oh, great Sun," squeaked Chip, bowing so low his nose touched his cheese sandwich. "We seek the strongest husband for Trixie!" The Sun chuckled. "Strongest, eh? Well, I appreciate that, but have you seen those clouds up there? They can block me out in a snap! Clouds are stronger than me!"

Surprised, Chip packed his picnic basket and with Trixie in tow, they climbed a beanstalk (the fastest way to reach the clouds). "Mighty Clouds," Chip squeaked, dodging a raindrop the size of a walnut, "will you marry Trixie? The Sun says you're the strongest!" The clouds rumbled sleepily. "Hmm, marry a little mouse? Flattering, but the Wind blows us around whenever he wants to. He's the real strong one!"

Off they went again, this time following a whistling tune, the Wind's song. They found him swirling through a field of wildflowers. "Powerful Wind," Chip called out, holding onto his hat. "We need the strongest husband for Trixie! The clouds say that's you!" The Wind whooshed around them, ruffling their fur. "Strongest? Have you seen that majestic castle over there? I've been trying to blow it down a hundred years now, but it just won't budge!"

Intrigued, Chip and Trixie followed the wind to the castle. "Oh, grand Castle," Chip squeaked, his voice barely a whisper against the walls. "Will you marry Trixie? The Wind says you're the strongest!" The castle's deep voice echoed through its halls. "Strongest?"

"Not quite! I am honored, but I am not the strongest. Do you hear the tiny roars within my walls? They are the sounds of mice chewing through me, and they will soon bring me down. The mice are the strongest." Chip's eyes widened. Back in their burrow, he looked at Trixie, who was giggling at their wild goose chase. "It appears," he said, "the strongest husband isn't the biggest or the flashiest. Maybe, it's the one who's kind, brave, and, well, enjoys cheese as much as you do!" And so, with her father's blessing, Trixie married a charming mouse who loved cheese just as much as she did. They lived happily ever after, proving that love is the strongest force of all!

Sometimes what you seek far and wide is right in front of you, where you first started.

A Sweet Defeat

Carry the Crumb Witch lived in a tower so dusty, even the cobwebs complained. Her one weird hobby? Spying on kids who loved eating candy and cackling with joy if she saw a single black tooth. That was because, secretly, Carry craved for the shiniest smile in the land, to be her own. Every morning, she would ask her cracked mirror, "Mirror, mirror, who's got the brightest teeth of all?" and the mirror always lied, saying, "You, Carry, with a smile brighter than the sun!"

However, one day, the mirror malfunctioned! "Kiara has the brightest, most beautiful smile I have ever seen!" it blurted, a little timidly and with a pinch of terror. Carry shrieked like a teakettle. "Kiara? Who's Kiara?! You never mentioned her before!" The mirror had to tell Carry everything about Kiara. She was threatening to throw it out the window.

Furious, Carry hatched a plan so rotten it would make your teeth ache. She disguised herself as a friendly granny and opened up a candy shop right next to Kiara's house. Her shelves overflowed with lollipops that changed colors, fizzy candies that tickled your nose, and chocolate so good it practically sang! It was every kid's paradise!

Inevitably, Kiara skipped in, her eyes as wide as saucers. "Wow! Can I have some of that chocolate?" Carry, disguised as Granny Gummy, smiled. "Absolutely, dear! Take all you want!" She even told Kiara that she didn't have to pay anything because she was such a good girl! Day after day, Kiara gobbled up candy like a hungry hamster. After all, it was free! Carry rubbed her bony hands together, picturing Kiara's smile turning into a graveyard of gray teeth. But weeks later, when Carry checked her mirror... "Kiara still has the most dazzling smile!"

Carry sputtered like a leaky faucet. "But... all that candy..." The mirror wheezed, "Kiara brushes her teeth after every meal, and flosses like a pro! Good habits beat sugary treats any day!" Carry stormed into her shop, disguise now gone. "Kiara! How?!" Kiara, brushing with a sparkly toothbrush, grinned. "My parents taught me to take care of my smile! Candy's nice, but healthy teeth are even better!" Carry, defeated by a toothbrush, stomped her foot. Soon, all the kids, inspired by Kiara's pearly whites, started brushing too. Carry's dream of rotten teeth vanished into thin air. Grumbling, she packed her bags and left, forever haunted by the memory of a sparkling smile and a toothbrush.

Good habits and self-care can protect you from harm, even when temptation is everywhere.

Mitzy's Choice

Mitzy the cat was definitely not an alley cat. Unlike her scrawny, whisker-twitching friends scavenging for scraps, Mitzy lived a life of luxury with Mr. Cooper, a human obsessed with healthy food. Every morning, it was toast and sunny-side up fried eggs, that looked like big bulging eyes. Lunch was a parade of colorful veggies and lean meat that smelled like... well, like healthy food. Dinner was sometimes fishy and sometimes beany, but always good for you, which, according to Mitzy, wasn't always fun.

Looking out the window, Mitzy often saw her street cat pals feasting on what looked like the most delicious things ever – greasy burgers, pizza dripping with cheese, and even ooey-gooey cupcakes! "Ugh," Mitzy thought, "Mr. Cooper with his 'whole wheat this' and 'lean protein that.' Where's the fun in healthy?" Until one day, Mr. Cooper announced, "Mitzy, I'm off to a conference about... well, you already know - healthy food! I'll be gone two weeks, but I've stocked your bowls!" He winked. "Don't get into any trouble!"

The second Mr. Cooper's car was out of sight, mischief became Mitzy's middle name. With a wiggle of her shiny pink nose, she darted outside. The neighborhood strays looked at her with suspicion, but the aroma of a half-eaten, discarded burger quickly won them over. Mitzy dug in – grease dripped down her chin, and pepperoni stuck to her fur. It tasted amazing! Day after day, Mitzy partied with the strays. Fries rained from the sky (okay, not really, but they were everywhere), and cupcakes were her new best friends. Delicious!

But slowly, things changed. Mitzy's sleek fur turned as dull as yesterday's newspaper, and her once playful jumps became sluggish waddles. Her belly grew rounder than a bouncy ball, and even squeezing through the cat door became a mission impossible. One evening, as the sun was diving below the houses, Mitzy felt a wave of regret.

Sitting outside, oversized and uncomfortable, she remembered Mr. Cooper's healthy meals and how good they made her feel. "Maybe freedom isn't worth feeling this awful," she thought. Just then, headlights rounded the corner. It was Mr. Cooper! Mitzy yowled, but all that came out was a weak meow. Mr. Cooper rushed over, his eyes widening at the sight of his formerly fit feline friend. Back home, Mr. Cooper put Mitzy on a healthy track again. It wasn't easy, but slowly, Mitzy's fur gleamed, her eyes sparkled, and her playful jumps returned. Mitzy learned a valuable lesson – sometimes, healthy isn't the most fun word, but it sure beats feeling like a furry bowling ball!

Healthy habits keep you feeling and looking good, even if unhealthy choices seem more fun at first.

Meet Nobody

Adam wasn't afraid of monsters under the bed. Oh no. He was afraid of the WHOLE DARK ROOM! Every night, when the lights went out, Adam's room turned into a jungle gym for shadows. Creaks became monster footsteps, and night breezes whooshed like ghosts whispering secret threats. One night, curled under his covers like a scared burrito, Adam saw a shadow that looked suspiciously like a bunny with a bad hair day. He squeezed his eyes shut, but then a tiny voice tickled his ear. "Hey there, scaredy-cat!"

Adam peeked out. There was... nobody there? "Who said that?" he squeaked. "It's me, Nobody," a giggle echoed. "I'm invisible like the darkness you fear, remember?" Suddenly, a warm hand grabbed Adam's hand and whoosh! They were flying! Up, up, and away from the scary shadows. The wind tickled his face as they soared over a field of flowers that glowed like neon signs. Fireflies blinked at them like fairy lights in a jar.

Next stop? A forest filled with the sound of rustling leaves! The wind whispered soft, mesmerizing songs, and owls hooted greetings. A fuzzy bunny with a twitchy nose hopped by, not scary at all, just curious. Adam even spotted a mama deer with her wobbly-legged fawn. The whole place was like a huge sleepover for adorable animals!

Their adventure continued over a glittery ocean. Dolphins jumped like acrobats, and Adam could swear he saw a mermaid's tail flash beneath the waves. Maybe mermaids wore glowing swimsuits at night? Finally, they flew over a village with houses all lit up like Christmas trees. Kids chased each other, their laughter filling the air. Grown-ups were gazing at the stars, dreaming of the endless galaxies. It looked like so much fun!

"Wow," whispered Adam, feeling braver than Superman. "See?" Nobody said. "The dark isn't scary, it's just full of adventures waiting to happen. Use your imagination, and you can go anywhere!" Back in his room, the shadows still danced on the walls, but Adam wasn't scared anymore. He knew they were just friendly night shapes. With a sleepy smile, Adam drifted off to dream of fireflies, baby deer, and maybe even a neon-swimsuit wearing mermaid. The dark wasn't something to fear, it was a secret door to a world of nighttime fun!

Imagination can turn fear into wonderful adventures; you are never truly alone.

Tough Night on the Farm

Oink! Oink! Poco the Pig squealed through the night, causing distress among the farm animals. He was having a night like a scratched record – full of loud, squeaky repeats. His snores had turned into snorts that echoed through the barn. By morning, everyone was cranky and concerned, a grumpy mess. Daisy the Duck, looking like she had just lost a feather pillow fight, waddled over to Poco. "Poco," she quacked, "what's the big squeal about? You sound like a teakettle about to explode!"

Poco, his face twisted in pain, could barely oink. "My tooth! It throbs like a jackhammer!" he managed. Daisy blinked. "Toothache? I wouldn't know. We ducks don't have teeth!" News travels fast on a farm, and Gertie the Goat trotted over. "A toothache? Oh no! Those are the worst! Feels like your head is trying to fly away!" The farmyard turned into a support group.

Benny the Rabbit hopped over with a mouthful of clover. "Grandma says this helps with pain!" Poco munched on the clover, but his squeals turned into high-pitched yips. "Nope, not working!" he cried. Millie the Cat, the mysterious one, sauntered over. "I remember reading about a toothache spell in a book," she muttered, waving her paws dramatically. But after a few weird cat noises and tail swishes, Poco's tooth still throbbed like crazy.

Just then, Bruno the Donkey, known for his big ideas, spoke up. "Wait a minute! Why don't we just pull the tooth out?" Everyone looked at Bruno, then back at Poco, whose eyes were wide with fear. "Okay but be gentle!" he squeaked. They tied a string to Poco's tooth and the other end to a fence post. "Hold still, Poco," Bruno instructed. But Poco, was so scared that he kept inching forward. The more they pulled, the more Poco scooted.

Bruno and his friend Barney the Donkey tried to hold him still, but Poco was a wiggly, oinky mess. Finally, exhausted and defeated, Poco blurted out, "Okay, okay! It's not my tooth!" The farmyard animals stared, confused. "Not your tooth?" Daisy repeated.

Poco shuffled his hooves and mumbled, "I ate too many green apples yesterday. You would call me greedy if I told you..." Bruno smiled kindly. "We all make mistakes, Poco. But honesty is the best medicine, even for a tummy ache! We could have made you some soothing chamomile tea instead of this crazy tooth-pulling rodeo!" Poco's tummy did feel a bit better already. The relieved animals helped him find some soothing food, and that night, the barn was finally quiet. Poco learned a valuable lesson: truth and a little help from friends are always better than a fake toothache!

> ✦ Always tell the truth, especially when you need help from your friends. ✦

A Magical Comeback

Alyssa the fairy was having a bad day. Flying? More like flopping. Spells? More like sputters and smoke puffs. Flowers? More like wilted weeds whenever she tried to help them bloom. Every day, she watched her friends flit around like fancy ballerinas, casting spells with a flick of their wrists. Alyssa just felt clumsy and, well, un-magical. One afternoon, Alyssa sat on a rock, chin in her hands. Kyra, her best friend, buzzed over. "Hey, Alyssa, why the long face?" Alyssa sighed. "I'm the worst fairy ever. I can't fly, my spells fizzle fast, and flowers turn droopy when I come near them. I'll never be as amazing as everyone else."

Kyra landed beside her, looking concerned. "That's not true, Alyssa. But I know what might cheer you up! Ever heard of a phoenix?" Alyssa shook her head, a flicker of curiosity peeking through her gloom. "Nope, what's that?" Kyra's eyes sparkled. "Imagine a magnificent bird, fiery and strong! It lives for ages, but when it gets old, it bursts into flames! Then, a new phoenix chick is born from the ashes! It's like a chance to be even stronger than before."

Alyssa's eyes widened. "Wow, that's incredible! But how does that help me?" Kyra nudged her with a wing. "Think about it! Every time you mess up a spell or trip while flying, it's like a tiny burst of fairy-dust ashes. And just like the phoenix, you can use that to start fresh, learn from your mistakes, and become better!" A flicker of hope ignited in Alyssa's eyes. "Do you really think so?" Kyra winked. "Absolutely! You have the spirit of a phoenix. Now, let's practice!" With Kyra's help, Alyssa started over.

Kyra showed her how to ride the wind currents. At first, Alyssa wobbled and nearly nose-dived into a daisy patch, but she remembered the phoenix and kept trying. Slowly, she started to glide, her laughter echoing through the forest. Next, they tackled spells. Kyra patiently showed Alyssa the right wand movements and magic fairy words to say. There were still a few smoke puffs, but sometimes a perfect shower of glittery bubbles erupted from her wand. Every little success made Alyssa feel like she could sprinkle fairy dust on the whole world.

Finally, they reached the flower garden. Kyra showed Alyssa how to focus her magic on the droopy blooms. Alyssa closed her eyes, picturing a strong, fiery phoenix chick, and then waved her wand. This time, the flowers perked up, their petals shimmering with newfound life. By the end of the week, Alyssa had transformed. She could fly with confidence, her spells worked, and the flowers bloomed at her touch. There were still stumbles here and there, but Alyssa didn't feel like a failure anymore. She was a phoenix in training, and with Kyra by her side, she knew she could achieve anything!

Never give up, even when you fail; every setback is a chance to start over and grow stronger.

Frodo's Close Call

Frodo the Frog was not an obedient school hopper. Sure, he loved learning about wiggly worms and fly-catching techniques, but sometimes... well, sometimes the classroom walls - and rules - felt like they were closing in. Today's field trip was to the Gliding Reed Pond, and Frodo was bursting with excitement. But Mrs. Franny, their wise tortoise teacher, kept pointing her bony finger at a patch of tall reeds. "Those reeds," she croaked, "are off-limits. Nasty hawk lives there, and frogs are his favorite pizza topping!" Frodo gulped. A hawk? Like a giant, feathery flyswatter? Super exciting, not scary at all.

So, as Mrs. Franny showed the ducklings how to do beak-dives for water bugs, Frodo couldn't resist. The reeds whispered secrets and adventure was calling his name. Hop, hop, hop! Frodo waddled towards the reeds, feeling like a brave explorer in a jungle of secrets. He imagined dodging laser beams (because reeds shot laser beams, right?) when suddenly, a giant shadow fell over him. "Uh oh," Frodo croaked, looking up way too late. A creepy-looking hawk, with beady eyes, swooped down and snatched Frodo in his scary talons! "Lunchtime!" the hawk declared, his voice like a rusty hinge.

Back at the pond, chaos erupted. Mrs. Franny, who was usually very calm, shouted, "We have to help Frodo, but we need a plan! Do not panic!" The other animals squeaked and squawked, but the hawk just scoffed. "This little hopper is mine!" Just then, a magnificent eagle named Tolk, the pond's superhero, flew over the hawk. " "Release the frog!" Tolk said, his voice like a foghorn. The hawk gulped. He wasn't messing with Tolk.

With a frustrated squawk, the hawk dropped Frodo, who landed with a plop in the pond. Shaking and slightly flat, Frodo hopped back to Mrs. Franny. "See, Frodo?" Mrs. Franny said firmly. "Rules are there to keep you safe, especially from laser-shooting reeds." Frodo hung his head. "Sorry, Mrs. Franny. No more exploring without permission." The rest of the trip was amazing, but Frodo stuck close to Mrs. Franny. He learned a valuable lesson that day: exploring was fun, but safety came first. As for laser-shooting reeds and jungles of secrets? Totally fictional...

Always be obedient and follow the school rules; they are there to keep you safe.

First Base

Lucas gripped his bright red glove like a scared puppy. Today was his first baseball game, and his tummy felt like a washing machine full of jitters. He took a deep breath, hoping he wouldn't strike out, looking like a goofy giraffe. The game began with a loud "CRACK!" as the batter whacked the ball. Lucas, outfield-ready, squinted at the sky, searching for the white dot. There it was! He spotted it! He sprinted after it, tongue sticking out in concentration. But oh no! His shoelace, a sneaky traitor, decided to untie itself at the worst moment. PLOP! Lucas went down like a sack of potatoes, and the ball sailed past, happy and free. The other team cheered – they had scored!

Lucas felt his face turn the color of his glove. He had messed up big time. His teammates shuffled over, looking defeated. But then, like a superhero landing with a "POOF!", Grandpa Joe appeared beside him. He winked and said, "Let's chat, Slugger!" Grandpa Joe, with a wide smile, sat Lucas down. "Guess what, champ?" he chuckled, "When I was a little firecracker like you, I fumbled the ball more times than a juggling clown! In my first game, I tripped over my own shoelace and let the winning run score. Yep, just like you!"

Lucas's eyes widened. "Really, Grandpa? Even you?" Grandpa Joe nodded, his mustache wiggling. "Yup! But you know what? I dusted myself off, practiced like a lion training his powers, and got better with every game. Remember, everyone strikes out sometimes. The trick is to learn from your mistakes and keep swinging for the fences!"

Lucas felt a warm feeling spread in his tummy, replacing the washing machine churning jitters. He wasn't the only one making mistakes! He shared Grandpa Joe's story with his teammates, and soon, everyone was giggling and remembering their own silly baseball blunders. They decided to practice extra hard, vowing to be the silliest, most awesome team ever, even if they didn't always win. Lucas learned that baseball wasn't just about winning, it was about having fun, working together, and maybe even tripping over your shoelace once in a while!

Everyone makes mistakes, but what matters is that we learn from them and keep trying.

A Lesson in Kindness

Michelle, Lucy, and Sarah were the glitter queens of their school. They had fancy clothes and gadgets that beeped like a robot choir. One day, during recess, they spotted Amber and Nancy, who were the exact opposite, by the swings. Amber's shirt had a flower that looked like it had lost a fight with a cat, and Nancy's backpack had a few too many patches. "Whoa," Michelle snickered, "did they lose a game of 'dress up like your grandma'?" Lucy and Sarah burst out laughing, like hyenas who had just inhaled helium.

Michelle sashayed over to Amber and Nancy, her nose held high. "Hey there, Raggedy Anne and Patchwork Pete! Where did you find those clothes, the lost and found?" Amber's cheeks turned red, and Nancy stared at her scraped-up shoes. "Leave us alone," Nancy mumbled, feeling like a tiny mouse surrounded by hungry cats. But Michelle wouldn't stop. Every day, it was like a never-ending bullying cycle. Name-calling, clothes-criticizing, book-knocking-over – it was enough to make anyone cry into their lunchbox.

The principal, Mrs. Green called Michelle, Lucy, and Sarah to her office. "There's been a rumor in school," she said, her voice strict. "Apparently, you three have been giving a hard time to Nancy and Amber." Michelle crossed her arms and pouted. "We were just, you know, playing around." Mrs. Green's smile vanished. "Bullying is no laughing matter," she said. "Tomorrow, you three will spend the entire day with the two girls. Maybe then you'll understand how they feel." Michelle groaned, but there was no escaping Mrs. Green's orders.

The next day, they found Amber and Nancy, who looked like they would rather be swallowed by a whale, than spend the day with that group. "Uh, we have to hang out with you guys," Michelle mumbled. Amber and Nancy blinked, then slowly nodded. They took Michelle and her friends to their favorite spot in the school yard. They played games, told jokes and even shared their secret stash of yummy cookies. Slowly, Michelle's frown turned upside down. Amber and Nancy, despite their not-so-fancy clothes, were fun to be around!

But then some other kids started pointing and whispering. "The meanies are hanging out with the newbies!" someone yelled. Michelle felt a hot flush creep up her cheeks – for the first time, she understood how awful it felt to be teased. By the end of the day, Michelle felt terrible. "I'm so sorry," she mumbled. "We had no idea how much our teasing hurt." Amber and Nancy looked at each other, then smiled. "It's okay," Amber said. "Just promise not to do it again. Being bullied feels horrible." Michelle nodded seriously. "Promise."

Treat others how you want to be treated; bullying hurts everyone, while being kind always wins.

Learn to Shine

Ollie the ostrich peered into the pond, feeling like a walking feather duster caught in a windstorm. His long neck dangled this way and that, his legs stuck out like wobbly stilts, and his feathers poofed out in a permanent state of surprise. Every other animal at school looked sleek and stylish – the zebras with their crisp stripes, the lions with their fluffy manes – and Ollie just felt... awkward. Every day, Ollie tried to hide his long neck, hunching over until he resembled a question mark with feathers.

But his best friends, Buck the bunny and Carla the cat, wouldn't let him stay gloomy. "Ollie, you're one of a kind!" squeaked Buck, hopping around him. "There's no other ostrich like you in the whole savanna!" Carla purred softly, rubbing against Ollie's leg. "Yeah, your feathers are so soft, and your legs can kick so high!" But Ollie wasn't convinced. At recess, he would hide behind termite mounds, feeling all gloomy.

One day, while moping under a baobab tree, Robby the raven with his shiny black feathers, cawed softly and landed beside him. "Why so sad, Feathers?" Robby said. Ollie sighed. "Everyone else looks incredible! I just look... like a feathery mess." Robby cocked his head and cawed thoughtfully. "I felt the same way when I was younger. My feathers, all black, weren't as flashy as a peacock's or as smooth as a hawk's. But then I learned a very important secret." "What's that?" Ollie perked up a bit. "Being beautiful comes from the inside, Feathers," Robby cawed. "It's about being a good friend, helping others, and feeling confident about who you are. When you love yourself, everyone else sees your awesomeness too!" Ollie thought about this. Maybe Robby was right.

That afternoon, he decided to join his friends for a game. At first, he felt like a clumsy bird, but soon he forgot about his looks and just had fun! His long legs helped him run fast, and his friends cheered him on like he was the fastest ostrich in Africa. The next day, it was talent show time! Buck and Carla nudged Ollie towards the stage. "Show everyone those fancy footwork moves!" Buck squeaked, twitching his whiskers.

Ollie gulped, but Robby's words echoed in his head. With a deep breath and his friends by his side, he strutted onto the stage. He started dancing, his long legs kicking high and his feathers fluffing out. The other animals watched in surprise, then started clapping and cheering. When the music stopped, Ollie felt so excited. He realized his friends and classmates didn't care about his feathers – they liked him for his talent and the joy he brought them. From that day on, Ollie held his head high, feathers puffed with pride. He learned that being yourself and sharing your unique talents with the world was the coolest thing an ostrich could do!

True beauty comes from within; embrace your unique qualities and let your inner light shine.

Big Feelings

Susan slumped at the kitchen table, chin resting on her fists like a defeated warrior. Her dad, the world's greatest (but busiest) inventor, had vanished on another top-secret mission – probably saving the planet from rogue socks or something. Without him around, everything felt gloomy. The sun hid behind the clouds and her smile vanished into thin air.

As she sat there moping, Susan accidentally launched a glass of milk into outer space (well, almost – it just hit the floor). "Ugh! Why is everything going wrong?!" she yelled, tears welling up in her eyes. Her mom, a master hugger with a bright, optimistic smile, swooped in. "Hey there, Super Sad. It's just a glass." "It's not just a glass, Mom!" Susan cried. "Everything feels so wrong without Dad!" Mom squeezed her tight. "I get it, sweetie. Missing Dad is no fun. But sometimes, when feelings get trapped inside, they become ugly monsters! Let's talk about it, okay?" Sniffling, Susan agreed.

As they cuddled on the couch, she whispered, "I miss Dad a LOT. He's always flying off on adventures! He's never around..." Mom winked. "Well, you can be an adventurer too! Here's how to fight the ugly monster: First, talk it out, like you're telling your best friend. You can even write it all down in a secret notebook!" Susan considered this. "Okay, but what if talking doesn't work?" "Then, unleash your inner breathing dragon!" Mom instructed. "Take a big, deep breath in through your nose, hold it for a count of three, and then slowly let it out like a fire-breathing dragon!" Susan giggled and tried it. Poof! The ugly monster felt a little smaller.

"Finally," Mom said, "find your happy ray! Maybe draw a picture for Dad or sing your silliest song. How about you start reading that exciting book your dad gave you on your birthday, so you can share all about it with him, when he gets home?"

Susan's eyes lit up. "Doing things you love helps chase the blues away!" Mom continued. "I'll draw a picture of us three playing in the snow, like we did on New Year's!" Susan said. Mom laughed. "Sounds super-awesome! Remember, feeling sad is okay, but there are ways to fight the ugly monster and feel a little brighter. And hey, you always have your super-powered mom by your side!" Susan squeezed her mom back. With a toolbox full of new tricks, she knew she could handle anything, even missing her super-inventor dad, for a little while.

It's okay to feel sad; talking about your feelings and doing things you love can help you feel better.

Real Friends

A crash echoed across the icy plains. Boba the penguin, belly flopping out of his morning stretches, squawked, "What in the world?" Next to him, Manny the snowman blinked his pebble eyes. "Sounds like trouble!" he whispered, his voice a concerned rumble. There, sprawled near their burrow, was Alby the albatross, his wing bent awkwardly. "Oofta!" Alby groaned. "Blizzard took a nasty swipe at me. My wing's hurting, and I can't fly!"

Boba waddled over, concern etched on his feathery face. "Don't worry, Alby! We'll get you fixed up." Manny, ever the planner, chimed in, "Dr. Wolly, the brainy blue whale, lives near Colin Island. He's the best doctor ever, but it's a long, wobbly trek." Alby's beak drooped. "Colin Island? Sounds promising, but I can't exactly waddle there." Boba puffed up his chest, a tiny penguin pride shining. "Leave it to us! We'll bring Dr. Wolly to you!"

Their journey was a hilarious mess. First, they tackled Slippery Slope. Boba went zooming down like a feathered rocket, landing with a PLOP! Luckily, Manny, strong and steady as a snowman should be, tossed him a rope and hauled him back up. Next, they braved the Frozen Ice Pillar Forest. The frozen pillars were like enormous icicles, making it hard to see. But Boba, with his sharp penguin peepers, spotted a tiny trail. They tiptoed through the maze, giggling as snowflakes dripped on their heads.

Finally, they reached Blizzard Bridge, a narrow path over a bottomless chasm. The wind howled like a hungry walrus. Boba, nimble and quick, scurried across first. Manny followed, wobbly as a jellybean, but Boba grabbed his wobbly arm just in time! Reaching the icy water near Colin Island, they bellowed with all their might, for Dr. Wolly. A big blue eye blinked open! Dr. Wolly agreed to follow them back.

With Dr. Wolly carrying them on his back, the trip felt like a cool summer swim, compared to their wild adventure. Back at their burrow, Alby chirped with relief. Dr. Wolly, a true-blue friend, fixed Alby's wing in a jiffy. Soon, Alby was flapping his wings happily. "Thanks, guys!" Alby hooted. "You're the best friends a bird with a sore wing could ask for!" Boba and Manny grinned. Even with all the wobbles and slips, they had saved their friend. And that, in the icy plains of Antarctica, was a cause for celebration – maybe with a nice fish snack for everyone!

True friends will go to great lengths to help each other, no matter how difficult the journey.

Barnyard Battle

Blaze the donkey stomped his hoof, sending a cloud of dust flying. "Hey, Oscar! That's MINE!" he brayed, pointing his fuzzy nose at a tiny pile of hay. Oscar, munching on the last strand, looked up with a sly grin. "Mine now," he mumbled through a mouthful of hay. Blaze puffed out his chest, making him look like a miniature horse. "No way! I saw it first!"

Oscar rolled his eyes, which wasn't easy for a donkey. "Of course you did, Mr. I-See-Everything Blaze. But I ate it first, so it's mine!" This wasn't the first time Blaze and Oscar, the best (and sometimes worst) of friends, had argued over something silly. Like who had the fluffiest tail (Blaze, obviously) or who could bray the loudest (always a tie). But this time, it was WAR... over the smallest, tiniest pile of hay! They circled each other, snorting and kicking their hooves. Blaze tried to nibble Oscar's tail, and Oscar attempted to trip Blaze with his giant fuzzy slippers (donkeys don't wear slippers but pretend with me)!

Just then, the barn door creaked open. Farmer Jack, with a very angry look on his face, stood in the doorway. "What's all this racket about?" he boomed. Blaze and Oscar froze, mid-kick and mid-nibble. "Uh... nothing, Farmer Jack," they mumbled together, their voices squeaking like scared mice. Farmer Jack sighed. "Nothing, huh? Sounds like a donkey riot in here. You two are supposed to be best friends, not sworn enemies!" Blaze and Oscar's ears drooped lower than their tails. "Go cool your hooves," Farmer Jack said, shaking his head. "You will stay in here, with no supper tonight, until you get to your senses! Maybe by morning, you'll remember how to share," he roared, slamming the barn door shut.

No supper for fighting? That was worse than no hay! Alone in the dusty barn, Blaze and Oscar's tummies grumbled like empty buckets. "Maybe we were a bit silly," Blaze mumbled. Oscar nodded, his long face drooping. "Yeah, a tiny hay fight wasn't worth missing supper." They bumped noses, a donkey's way of apologizing. "Friends?" Blaze asked. "Friends," Oscar agreed. Curled up together for warmth, their empty bellies a reminder of their silliness, they dreamed of a breakfast of fluffy hay and maybe even a few extra carrots for being such good friends (once again).

Fighting over small things can lead to big consequences; it's better to share and work together.

Ronnie and Red

Ronnie the rooster and Red the dog were the farm's best adventure buddies. They would chase butterflies together, nap in sun puddles warmer than any blanket, and explore the woods like fearless superheroes. One afternoon, they chased a butterfly so dazzling it looked sprinkled with glitter. They chased and chased, deeper and deeper into the woods, until... the sun dipped below the trees, as darkness started to settle, giving way for the moonlight to fill the night sky.

"Uh oh," Ronnie clucked, his feathers standing on end like a worried haystack. "It's getting dark, Red! How will we ever find our way back?" Red, the smartest dog on four legs (at least, that's what he thought), spotted a big oak tree with a cozy hollow at its base. "Don't fret, Ronnie," he woofed. "You perch on a branch, and I'll snuggle up in the hollow. We'll be back at the farm tomorrow." Ronnie hopped onto a sturdy branch, and Red curled up inside the hollow. They were about to drift off to sleep when... a loud crow shattered the forest silence. "Cock-A-Doodle-Doo!" Ronnie crowed, announcing midnight. He couldn't help it; it was in his nature.

Miles away, Vera the fox, with a nose for trouble and a taste for roosters, perked up her ears. "A rooster in the forest? Jackpot!" she cackled, her eyes glowing. She crept towards the sound, her fluffy tail swishing with anticipation. Reaching the tree, Vera saw Ronnie perched high above. "My, what a beautiful voice!" she cooed in her sweetest tone. "Come down, handsome rooster, and let me give you a hug for that lovely crowing!"

Ronnie, not falling for her foxy tricks, replied, "Thank you, kind fox! But I can't climb down. My doorman has to open the tree door first." Vera, picturing another delicious rooster, eagerly approached the hollow. "Doorman? Wake up, sleepyhead! A handsome rooster needs his door opened!" Suddenly, with a bark that could wake the dead, Red burst out of the hollow! "Woof! Woof! Go bother a different forest, you sneaky fox!" Vera's eyes widened. With a yelp, she turned tail and ran as fast as she could, Red hot on her heels, barking all the way.

"Dog alert! Dog alert!" she yelped, disappearing into the trees. Red chased her until she was a tiny dot, then trotted back to the tree, panting but proud. "Nice thinking, Ronnie! You outsmarted that foxy trickster!" Ronnie fluffed his feathers with a chuckle. "Teamwork makes the dream work, Red! After all, who needs a boring old doorman when you have a super dog-man?" As the first rays of sunshine peeked through the trees, the two friends made their way back to the farm, their hearts full of relief. From that day on, they stuck a little closer to home, knowing that together, they could face any adventure — even a midnight encounter with a hungry fox!

Teamwork and quick thinking can help you outsmart even the trickiest of problems.

Lost in the City

Henry Grayhood, the tiniest, twitchiest mouse in his family of ten, was having a case of wanderlust. "Big City, here I come!" he squeaked, packing his imaginary knapsack (mice don't carry knapsacks, but use your imagination). His parents, Mama and Papa Grayhood, exchanged worried whisker-twitches. "The city is... well... a bit too much. I don't think you will like it there." Mama squeaked. But Henry, full of dreams of cheese mountains and pastry palaces, set off with a spring in his step and a map drawn on a borrowed, sunflower seed.

After a long journey (mostly dodging farm cats and curious chickens), Henry reached the Big City. Cars honked like angry geese, buildings scraped the clouds, and the sheer number of SCENTS made his tiny nose twitch with excitement. He finally found an open bakery door. It felt like hitting the jackpot! Slipping inside, Henry's eyes widened. Rows upon rows of glistening croissants, mountains of crumbly bread, and a giant cheese wheel that looked as big as the moon! He started building his nest behind a flour sack when...

With the corner of his eye, he caught a flash of black fur! A sleek cat with eyes like emeralds stalked towards him. Henry, heart hammering in his chest, saw the cat's reflection in a silver spoon. With a squeak, he leaped out of the way just as the cat pounced! Chaos erupted. The cat chased Henry through the bakery, sending flour flying and pastries tumbling. Henry dodged rolling pins and leaped over surprised chefs, finally escaping through a hole in the wall. Breathless and covered in flour, Henry looked around the noisy city.

It didn't feel like the cheese palace of his dreams anymore. "Maybe safe and sound is better than plenty and frightening," he squeaked, missing his cozy corner back home. Henry raced back to his familiar barn, his heart yearning for home. His family, relieved and happy, welcomed him with squeaks and snuggles. Curled up next to his parents, Henry realized the richest treasure wasn't cheese mountains, but the love and safety of his family. From then on, Henry never complained about the farm again. After all, who needs giant cheese wheels when you have a family who loves you truly?

Being happy does not mean having plenty; it's being safe and having people you love nearby.

The Impatient Tree

Up on a snowy mountain peak lived a little almond tree, named Aria. Unlike the other trees all snuggled together in the cozy valley below, Aria stood alone, shivering in the cold wind. Each year in February, she would peek down and see her sister Bella, surrounded by buzzing bees and boasting the most beautiful pink blossoms you had ever seen.

One day, the sun shortly peeked out of the clouds, and it melted some snow, revealing a tiny patch of green. "Spring is here!" Aria declared, even though snowflakes were still clinging to her branches. "Time to bloom!" Jill, the oldest almond tree on the mountain, was wiser than that. She saw Aria's eagerness and chuckled, her bark creaking like an old rocking chair. "Hold on there, little sprout," Jill rasped. "These mountain winds are no joke. Bloom too early, and your flowers will be blown away sooner than you think!"

But Aria, stubborn as a mule, ignored her. She pushed and prodded her branches until, poof! Tiny pink flowers sprouted, making her feel like a million butterflies had tickled her branches. She looked so beautiful! For a few days, Aria was the happiest tree on the mountain. But then... a gray storm cloud, suddenly unleashed its fury. The wild wind whipped through the mountains, howling like a hungry wolf. Aria clung to her flowers for dear life, but the wind was too strong. Pink petals went flying like confetti in a crazy squirrel party!

By the time the storm settled, and the wild wind calmed down, Aria was completely bare. No flowers, no bees, and definitely no almonds that year. Breathless, Aria looked down at her branches. Tears welled up in her little trunk and a shiver ran through her roots.

Jill, put a comforting branch around Aria. "See, young one? What did I tell you? Patience is like a delightful bowl of almonds – it takes time to get it right!" Aria, feeling quite depressed, nodded solemnly. "You're right, Jill. From now on, I'll wait for the perfect time to bloom." And so, the next spring, Aria waited patiently. When the wind calmed and the sun shone brightly, she bloomed later than everyone else. But guess what? Her flowers were the strongest and most beautiful yet! Aria learned a valuable lesson: good things come to those who wait, especially when you're a little almond tree on a windy mountaintop!

Wait for the right time to do something; rushing into things can lead to disappointment.

Catching Garry

Garry the Wolf had a rumbling tummy problem. Not the kind you get from eating too many cookies (though he wouldn't say no to that), but the kind that comes with having two very hungry cubs at home. One afternoon, Garry peeked over the edge of the forest and spotted Farmer Tony's farm. Now, Tony wasn't the smartest farmer around. His fence was shorter than his own knees, and his guard dog, Snoozer, spent most days napping like a champion slug. In the middle of the field stood a plump, tasty-looking goat – practically begging to be a wolf's lunch!

Garry, known for being an opportunist, snatched the goat with a sneaky grin. "Problem solved!" he chuckled, dashing off towards the forest with his prize. Back at the farm, Tony stomped his feet and made a racket you could hear all the way to next Tuesday. "That pesky Garry!" he yelled. "He won't get away with this!" He gathered all the other farmers, who, truth be told, weren't much braver than scaredy-cats. Armed with pitchforks and water guns (because real rifles seemed a bit too much for a stolen goat), they marched into the forest, determined to catch Garry.

Now, Garry was no stranger to the forest. He zipped and zagged through the trees, leaving the farmers tripping over their own feet and arguing about who had the worst sense of direction. Days turned into weeks, and the farmers were exhausted. Their bellies rumbled louder than a hungry bear, and their only trophy was a collection of itchy mosquito bites.

Meanwhile, back in the village, everyone was worried sick. Finally, a search party found the lost farmers, who stumbled back home looking more like tired raisins than fierce hunters. The wise village elders gathered everyone. "Chasing Garry through the woods is like trying to catch a greased watermelon," they said.

"Instead, let's build fences so tall even a giraffe would need a ladder!" The farmers, though stubborn, knew this was the right thing to do. Soon, the village was bustling with activity. Up went extra-tall fences, and in trotted a pack of fierce guard dogs, with ears that perked up at the slightest sound. The village finally felt safe, and Garry learned to respect a good fence. He still found delicious food in the forest, but the well-guarded farms were a no-go zone. After all, a clever wolf knows when to pick his battles, especially when they involve angry farmers and very aggressive guard dogs!

Instead of chasing after problems, focus on finding solutions that prevent them in the first place.

Space Adventure

Benjamin, an experienced astronaut with a million space miles under his belt, was rocketing towards a brand-new planet called Cyclo. This time, he wasn't alone. Buckle up, because his copilot was his son, William, a fearless little dude who loved everything space related. Cyclo was unlike anything they had ever seen. The sky was bright blue, like a big swimming pool, and the ground glowed with funky purple plants. Benjamin, his crew, and William hopped out to explore, bouncing a little because Cyclo's gravity was weird.

Suddenly, enormous aliens with glittery scales and way too long arms rounded a corner. They looked like they belonged on a pizza – in a scary way! The aliens gripped glow-sticks, probably not for a party, and stared at the visitors with laser-beam eyes. Yikes! Before anyone could yell "aliens!", William, even though his knees were trembling, remembered his dad's stories about always being friendly in awkward situations. Taking a deep breath, he stuck out his hand, palm open, like a high-five for the biggest alien and smiled.

The aliens blinked, their glow-sticks dimming a bit. Confused, the tallest one, who looked like the boss alien, kneeled very carefully, and gently touched William's hand with one of his long, scaly fingers. Suddenly, a beepy machine whirred to life. "Welcome, little visitors! We are the Cyclarri. Why are you here?" it translated in a squeaky, robotic voice. Benjamin and his crew sighed with relief. "We come in peace!" said Benjamin through the machine. "We're explorers from Earth, just checking out your spectacular planet!" The boss alien, who introduced himself as Zig, smiled (well, at least they thought it was a smile – it looked a bit like a grimace) and asked them to follow.

As it turned out, the Cyclarri were quite nice once you got to know them. They showed William and his dad amazing crystal cities, robots that walked dogs, and gardens filled with plants that smelled like hot chocolate! All because William wasn't afraid to say hello! They learned that even across galaxies, friendship can start with a simple wave and a lot of bravery. When it was time to go, the Cyclarri waved them goodbye, promising to write, although space mail is notoriously slow! As their spaceship rocketed back to Earth, William knew this adventure was one giant leap to awesome!

A simple smile can go a long way; even when things seem scary, be brave and try to be friendly.

Reach for the Stars

Nelson the sloth had a big dream – to touch the brightest star in the sky! Every night, he would hang upside down from his favorite branch, drooling a little and gazing up at his starry friend. Now, Nelson wasn't exactly the most, well, sleek creature. He was slow, sleepy, and his attempts to reach the star were, shall we say, hilarious. First, he tried a twig and vine ladder. It looked impressive, for a sloth-built ladder. But halfway up, with Nelson clinging on for dear life, the whole thing went sproing! Nelson ended up dangling upside down again, but this time a little closer to the ground.

Next, inspired by a graceful toucan, Nelson used a giant leaf as a parachute. He climbed to the highest branch, took a deep breath, and leaped! But instead of soaring like a bird, Nelson went splat on his back with a "boing!" Then came the banana-leaf kite. Nelson tied himself to it, dreaming of a gentle breeze carrying him to the stars. He ran as fast as his sloth legs could go, but the kite just flopped and landed him in a bush full of annoyed bugs.

Feeling defeated, Nelson sat under his tree, staring sadly at the star. Suddenly, Coco the monkey swung by. "Hey, Slowpoke," she chirped, "what's wrong?" Nelson sighed and told her about his dream and all his epic fails. Coco, being a very optimistic monkey, grinned. "Why not climb the tallest tree in the forest? Maybe that'll get you closer! Follow me!" With Coco swinging from branch to branch, Nelson slowly followed, finally reaching the very top. The view was amazing, but the star was still very far away.

Just then, Hank the hawk circled by. "What's going on up here?" he asked. Nelson explained his dream, and Hank chuckled. "Hop on," he said, offering his back. Up, up they flew, but even Hank couldn't quite reach the star. As they soared through the sky, a majestic eagle, Rowan, spotted them. Hearing Nelson's story, Rowan offered a ride even higher. They kept going higher and higher, with different amazing birds offering help, but the star remained just out of reach. Finally, they met Casey, a majestic condor with a huge wingspan!

Casey listened patiently and then said, "I can take you the highest anyone has ever flown." Nelson climbed onto Casey's back, and they soared higher than the clouds, higher than he ever imagined. The air grew thin, and the stars twinkled like a million diamonds. Finally, Casey slowed down, and Nelson stretched out his paw. With a smile that stretched from ear to ear, he touched the brightest star! A warm, sparkly feeling filled him with pure joy. Nelson's dream came true, thanks to his amazing friends who helped him reach for the stars!

Never give up on your dreams; with good friends by your side, the sky is the limit.

Never-Ending Tale

King Rupert adored bedtime stories. Not just any stories, mind you. He craved never-ending tales that could last from breakfast all the way to bath time. He would sit on his enormous throne, surrounded by mountains of fluffy pillows, listening to historians drone on about brave knights and fire-breathing dragons. But the problem was, every story had to end eventually, which left King Rupert feeling depressed. "There must be a story that never ends!" he would complain, his voice echoing through the castle walls.

Determined to find this magical story, King Rupert announced a competition fit for a (slightly spoiled) king. "Whoever tells me a story that never ends will get half my kingdom!" he declared. "But beware, storytellers! If your tale ends and I'm not snoring happily, you'll be spending the night in the castle dungeon!" Eager to win such a generous prize, many storytellers flocked to the palace. The first storyteller managed to captivate the king for three months straight, with his intricate tales of dragons and magic. But eventually, he became confused, mixed up his words, and the story came to an abrupt end. The king, disappointed and angry, sent him to prison. Seeing the fate of the first competitor, the other storytellers fled the kingdom, leaving the king's challenge unmet.

Months passed, and the king's sadness deepened, until one day, a foreigner named Hudson arrived at the palace gates. "I will tell you a story that never ends," Hudson proclaimed confidently. Intrigued, the king welcomed him into the grand hall, where Hudson began his tale. "There was once a great king," Hudson started, "who had vast stores of wheat in his kingdom. One day, a terrible plague of ants descended upon the land. The ants devoured every seed they could find, leaving the fields barren. But then they discovered the king's storage house, filled to the brim with wheat." The king leaned forward, eager to hear more.

Hudson continued, "The ants searched tirelessly for a way into the storage house. Finally, they found a tiny hole, just large enough for one ant to squeeze through. And so, the first ant entered, picked up a single grain of wheat, and took it outside. Then the second ant went in, took a grain, and came out. After that, the third ant went in..." Hudson's tale progressed in this way, describing each ant's journey in meticulous detail.

Days turned into weeks, and weeks into months. The king was captivated, listening intently as Hudson described the endless procession of ants. After two years had passed, the king, now exasperated, interrupted, "How many more ants are there? When will they finish?" Hudson smiled and replied, "There are millions of ants, Your Majesty, and we have only just begun. They barely took out a small portion of the king's wheat." Realizing the genius of Hudson's never-ending story, the king laughed. "Enough! I am defeated. You have won, Hudson. Your tale has no end, just as you promised."

Creativity and perseverance can turn even the simplest ideas into something extraordinary.

Odin's Mother

Beatrice the mama hen had five fluffy chicks following her around the farm. But one chick, Odin, was the star of the show! She was a puffball of black feathers with eyes that sparkled. Beatrice loved them all, but Odin, well, she held a special place in her wing. Now, Odin was a curious chick. She would waddle up to the cow, Bessie, and ask her about the best grass-eating spots and would chat with Gary the goat about the tastiest weeds. But one farmyard friend was off-limits – Bob the cat. Beatrice had warned Odin a million times (that is a lot of clucking) to stay away from that furry gossip.

One afternoon, Beatrice was busy showing her little chicks how to find the juiciest worms, when Odin spotted Bob napping under the apple tree. Driven by curiosity, she tiptoed closer and squeaked, "Hi there, Mr. Fancy-Whiskers!" Bob opened one eye slowly. "Well, well," he drawled, licking his paw with a pink tongue. "Haven't seen you around before, chicky-poo." "My mama doesn't let me near you," peeped Odin, a little nervous. Bob's whiskers twitched. "Mama, huh? That old biddy isn't really your mama, you know." Odin's eyes widened. "What do you mean?" "The eggs you and your brothers came from? Taken from the farm next door," Bob smirked, a glint in his eye. "She just kept you warm until you hatched. Not a real mama, huh?" Odin's little heart sunk. Confused and sniffly, she wandered off.

She bumped into Clara, an old hen with a bright red comb. "What's wrong, little one?" Clara clucked, noticing Odin's sad face. Odin spilled everything; her voice wobbly. Clara clucked sympathetically, then looked at Odin with gentle eyes. "I don't know if Beatrice is your real mama in the way that cat said," Clara started, "but let me tell you something that is far more important. Beatrice kept you warm and safe when you were just a white egg. She never left your side, not even for a sip of water!"

"She showed you where to find yummy worms and protected you from the rooster's pecks. Remember when that scary hawk swooped down? She chased him away, protecting her chicks at all costs!" Odin listened, her little heart warming up again. "So, if she's not my mama like Bob says, what is she?" she asked. Clara smiled. "She's your mama in the most important way. A mama loves you and takes care of you, no matter where you came from." Odin waddled back to the coop and snuggled under Beatrice's wing, feeling safe and loved. "Mama," she peeped, "I love you the most!" Beatrice fluffed her feathers and clucked softly. "I love you too, my little chickadee!"

A real mom (or dad) is someone who makes sacrifices, loves and takes care of you, no matter what.

Winter Blues

Ralph the hedgehog poked his head out of his burrow. Brrr! Everything was buried under a huge white blanket – the grass, the flowers, even Ralph's favorite shortcut across the field! He slumped back down, his quills drooping. "Ugh, winter is the worst," he grumbled. His dad, Harold, poked his head in. He was in a good mood, with a twinkle in his eye, even in the gloomy winter weather. "Looking defeated, son," he chuckled. "What's wrong?" "Everything is so white outside, Dad. It's so boring," Ralph complained. "I miss the sunshine, the flowers, all the fun stuff!" Harold snorted, a puff of air tickling Ralph's nose.

"Hold on there, spiky speedster! You're just not seeing the whole picture." Ralph perked up. "There's another picture?" Harold winked. "Of course! Winter is like a giant sleepover for everything outside. See all that snow? It's like a big fluffy blanket, keeping all the little seeds and sleepy flowers warm and cozy." Ralph's frown turned upside down. "Really? Like a seedy pajama party?" "Exactly!" exclaimed Harold. "Those tiny flowers are tucked in tight, dreaming about the day they'll bloom and paint the world with bright colors. The grass is taking a snooze, getting ready to turn into the greenest grass ever, for you to zoom around on!"

Ralph squealed with delight. He imagined tiny flowers in fuzzy slippers and sleepy blades of grass snoring softly. "Wow! Winter sounds kind of cool then!" "It gets even better," Harold continued. "The trees are having a nap too, but they're busy planning all sorts of green, shiny leaves to shade you from the summer sun. It's like nature is sleeping, getting ready for an exciting spring party!" Ralph's eyes sparkled. "So, the snow is like a secret code for spring?" Harold ruffled Ralph's quills. "Exactly! It's like a big 'shhh, getting ready for something awesome' message. And when spring finally arrives, it'll be the best one ever because everything will be so excited to finally wake up!"

Ralph wiggled with excitement. Winter wasn't just boring anymore; it was a secret waiting to unfold! He looked out at the snowy field with a new feeling. "Thanks, Dad!" he chirped. "I can't wait for the first swallow to chirp and wake up all the sleepy flowers!" Harold smiled. "Me neither, spiky speedster. Me neither." Inside their cozy burrow, Ralph snuggled close to his dad, dreaming of spring parties and the amazing adventures that awaited them, when the snow melted away. Winter wasn't so bad after all – it was just the beginning of something even better!

Patience and a different perspective help us see the hidden beauty in everything; good things take time.

The Magic Mirror

Tucker the Golden Retriever had explored every corner of his house, more than once! However, one afternoon, his nose led him to something new. A big, shiny surprise in the living room – a mirror taller than a whole stack of pancakes! Tucker froze. There, inside the mirror, staring right back at him, was another golden dog – a total copycat, with a wagging tail that went WHAP-WHAP, just like his did. This new friend tilted his head when Tucker did and jumped left when Tucker jumped left. It was like playing with his long-lost, fluffy twin! "Where did my humans discover him?" he was wondering.

Determined to make a new best bud, Tucker crouched low, his fluffy butt wiggling with excitement. But guess what? The other dog did the same! They both launched themselves at each other, noses meeting in a hilarious "boop" against the cold, hard mirror. "Blargh!" Tucker yelped, surprised. Where was the warm, squishy playmate? Confused, he unleashed his secret weapon: the Turbo-Tail Wag! He spun in circles, his tail a golden blur, leaving a mini-tornado of fur in his wake. But the mirror-dog just copied him, tail wagging so fast it looked like a propeller about to take flight! Next, Tucker launched "Operation Belly Rub." He rolled onto his back, presenting his fuzzy tummy for some serious belly scratches. The copy-dog? He rolled over too, legs flailing in the air like a happy beetle!

This was getting weirder by the minute! Finally, Tucker unleashed his ultimate attack: the Mega-Zoomies! He dashed around the room, barking and leaping like a furry rocket. The mirror-dog? He zoomed too, bumping into furniture and leaving a trail of disaster behind him. The living room looked like a war zone of adorable fluff! Panting and a little dizzy, Tucker stopped. The mirror-dog stopped too. They both stared at each other, tongues lolling out. Then, like a light bulb flickering on, it hit Tucker! This was not another dog! It was HIM!

He couldn't believe he had been playing with his own reflection all this time! He let out a happy bark (a little sheepish this time), realizing he had gotten a little carried away without using his super sniffer. Tail wagging, Tucker trotted away, feeling a bit silly but also super smart. He learned a valuable lesson that day: sometimes things aren't exactly what they seem at first sniff. It's always best to take a closer look before launching yourself at a mirror! So next time you see something strange, remember Tucker the Golden Retriever! Don't jump to conclusions, use your super brain power to figure things out!

Don't jump to conclusions when you see something new; always check things out first!

Children of the Year

Have you ever wondered why the seasons change? It's not magic, it's the Children of the Year! These four siblings holding hands, dance around the Earth, keeping the seasons in perfect rhythm. And they never get tired! Spring bursts onto the scene first, a walking explosion of flowers in every color imaginable. As Spring skips across the land, the air fills with the sweet scent of blooming roses, the gentle buzz of busy bees, and the chirping symphony of birds welcoming the warm breeze. Sleepy bears lumber out of their caves, squirrels gather acorns, and baby bunnies hop out to explore the world. Kids race through fields of wildflowers, chase butterflies and celebrate Easter with baskets of colorful eggs.

Summer arrives next, bringing warmer days! His wild dance moves bring scorching sunshine, that stretches the days into endless adventures. Lawns transform into veggie gardens overflowing with juicy tomatoes, plump strawberries, and crunchy cucumbers. The air hums with the buzz of cicadas and the sweet smell of sizzling burgers and hot dogs, drifting from backyards everywhere. Kids spend their days having water balloon fights and building sandcastles that rival medieval fortresses. Ice cream trucks jingle their happy tunes, and the nights crackle with the colors of Fourth of July fireworks.

Autumn shuffles in next. As he sways and shuffles, leaves transform in colors of red, orange, and gold, blanketing the ground in a crunchy carpet. The air crisps up, perfect for cozy sweaters and hot apple cider. The scent of pumpkin spice lattes fills the air, while kids go back to school with backpacks full of new crayons and notebooks, ready to learn and explore. Halloween night arrives, a spooky yet exciting parade of costumed creatures – giggling witches, soaring superheroes, and maybe even a runaway taco or two! Houses twinkle with jack-o'-lanterns, and the delicious smell of roasting marshmallows fills the air, as families gather around bonfires to share spooky stories.

Finally, Winter waltzes in like a snow angel. With each graceful twirl, snowflakes swirl down, blanketing the world in a pristine white wonderland. The smell of pine trees fills the air, while kids bundle up in cozy snow clothes, build snowmen and race down snowy hills on sleds, leaving trails of laughter in their wake. Steaming mugs of hot cocoa warm them up, as families gather around to celebrate Christmas. Twinkling lights, mountains of presents, and enough family snuggles to last a lifetime. So yeah, the Children of the Year, dance their way through the seasons, reminding everyone that each part of the year is filled with its own unique memories waiting to be made!

Each season has its own special gifts; enjoy and appreciate the beauty of nature.

True Beauty

Celeste the Peacock strutted through the forest like a walking rainbow. Her feathers were a dazzling explosion of blues, greens, and golds, each one sparkling like a tiny mirror catching the sun. When she fanned her tail out, it was a spectacular sight – totally awesome! One afternoon, Celeste spotted Apollo the Nightingale perched on a branch. This little brown bird wasn't much to look at, but as soon as he opened his beak, magic happened! Out came the most beautiful song you had ever heard. It was like a million tiny music boxes playing at once, making butterflies do pirouettes and squirrels stop mid-nut-stash to listen.

Celeste, however, wasn't exactly doing a happy dance. "Humph," she muttered to herself, "They all love his silly song, but no one notices my FABULOUS feathers! They're practically glowing like a sunset dipped in glitter!" Puffing out her chest like a blowfish, she stomped over to Apollo. "Hey birdie," she said, her voice dripping with fake sweetness, "why don't you see how plain you look compared to me? I mean, have you seen your twig legs and boring brown feathers?" Apollo stopped singing and tilted his head.

"Well, Celeste," he chirped, "it's true that you are pretty dazzling. Like a walking fireworks show! But have you ever tried singing? It might come out more like a mouse squeaking than anything else." Celeste stood there surprised. "What do you mean?" Apollo smiled. "Look, Celeste, everyone has something special. Your feathers look like you just walked out from some fancy party, but my song makes everyone feel happy inside. True beauty isn't just about how you look, it's also about how you make others feel."

Celeste thought for a moment. Maybe Apollo was right. Her feathers were amazing, but they couldn't make the whole forest want to sing along, like his songs did. The forest needed both sparkly feathers, but also some happy tunes! From that day on, Celeste and Apollo became the best of friends. Whenever Apollo sang his heart out, Celeste would spread her magnificent feathers, making the whole forest happy with what they heard and saw. They learned that being different was great and sharing your unique gifts with others was even better. After all, the world would be a pretty boring place if we all looked the same.

Everyone has a special gift; true beauty is found in what we bring to the world.

The King's New Taste

King Reginald the Rich wasn't like most kings. Sure, he had a magnificent castle, a spectacular crown, and enough jewels to fill a bathtub! But there was one problem – King Reginald was a picky eater. He only ate the fanciest, most expensive food. Truffles the size of tennis balls and golden-dusted asparagus? Absolutely! But anything even remotely normal, like, say, an onion? Forget about it! Until one day, a villager named Bruno the Baker was chatting with his neighbor and found out about it. "The king has never even tasted an onion!"

Bruno's eyes lit up. Onions? In the land of fancy feasts? This was his golden ticket! Bruno piled his cart high with the roundest, juiciest onions he could find. He marched right up to the castle guards, who looked at him like he was delivering a cart of exploding grenades. Inside the throne room, Bruno bowed low (almost tripping over his oversized flour-dusted shoes) and declared, "Your Majesty, I present a rare and exotic treat – the mighty onion!"

King Reginald, bored of his usual fancy food, perked right up. "An 'onion'? What in the kingdom is that?" The royal chefs, faces pale as undercooked dough, tried to stop Bruno, but it was too late. The onions sizzled in the pan, filling the room with a smell that made the king's nose crinkle. Finally, the dish arrived. The king took a bite, his eyes watering a little and then... his face lit up with excitement! "This is amazing!" he declared, tears streaming down his cheeks (from laughter, not the onions... probably). The king ordered his servants to empty the cart of the onions and replace them with gold. Bruno left the castle a happy, rich man.

News of Bruno's fortune reached his greedy brother, Bruce the Braggart, who had always envied his brother. "Onions, huh?" Bruce scoffed. "The king probably has never tasted garlic either!" He piled his cart with the strongest garlic he could find, sure he would be richer than Bruno in no time. At the palace, Bruce approached the king with respect, bowing his head slightly before finally presenting his garlic with a flourish. The king, still a little teary-eyed from the onions, took a bite.

This time, his face turned redder than a royal tomato! But instead of gold, the king's servants started filling Bruce's cart... with onions! "Onions?" Bruce sputtered. "But the garlic!" The king chuckled. "My dear Bruce, onions are my biggest treasure. So, I share that treasure with you!" Bruce slunk away, his cart overflowing with onions, a reminder that greed is a recipe for a smelly surprise. From that day on, King Reginald still loved fancy food, but he also learned to appreciate a little variety and maybe keep some nose plugs handy for his royal chefs!

Appreciate what you have and don't be jealous; good things come from honest efforts.

Mr. Nobody

Troublemakers! That's what everyone called Joe and Chris. These two brothers were like walking tornadoes, leaving a trail of giggles and disaster wherever they went. Their secret shield? Mr. Nobody! Mr. Nobody, according to them, was an invisible guy who loved causing chaos. One afternoon, their cousin Mary came over to play. Joe and Chris, eyes sparkling with mischief, decided Mr. Nobody needed some exercise. Crash! A glass vase shattered in the kitchen. "Who did this?" yelled Mom. "Nobody!" they chorused, wearing their most innocent smiles. Mom wasn't buying it, but they stuck to their story.

Next, they snuck up on Mary, armed with a bucket of water. Splash! Mary shrieked, her brand-new dress now looking like a drowned cat. The boys doubled over with laughter, pointing their fingers at thin air. "What happened here?" shouted Mom again. "We don't know. We saw Nobody!" they teased. Even the family cat, Molly, wasn't safe! Joe snuck up behind her, letting out a loud "Boo!" that sent poor Molly flying, while Chris watched and giggled. In her panic, she knocked over a flower vase, sending colorful flowers flying like confetti. "See? Mr. Nobody messes with everyone!" they said, trying (and failing) to look innocent.

Their pranking spree continued. They pretended to be pirates, their plastic swords clashing with a deafening clang. Dishes shattered on the floor and Mom came rushing in, her face full of frustration. "Nobody gets to play pirates in the house!" she yelled. But of course, the boys just pointed their fingers and said, "He snuck in again!" Finally, things went too far. They put a sharp toy on their baby brother's chair. The poor little guy sat on it with a yelp, tears welling up in his big eyes. Joe and Chris, pretending concern, rushed over. "Are you ok?" they said. But their act was fooling no one. Their mom gathered them both for a serious talk.

"Boys," she said, her voice firm, "this Mr. Nobody sounds an awful lot like... you two." The brothers looked down at their shoes, their cheeks burning red. "There's no such thing as Mr. Nobody," she continued. "It's time to take responsibility for your actions. Pranks are only funny when everyone's laughing, not crying." Joe and Chris finally understood. They apologized to everyone, from Mary's soggy dress to their tearful brother's sore bottom. They promised to mend their ways and ditch the Mr. Nobody excuse for good. After cleaning up, they learned that being honest and kind was way more fun than blaming an imaginary somebody for their messes. And let's just say, Mr. Nobody was never seen (or heard from) again!

Be honest and take responsibility for your actions; blaming others for your mistakes makes things worse.

Bragging Bart

February wind howled outside but beneath a cozy greenhouse, two tiny bugs buzzed with life. Bart the Fly, a braggart with a shiny black body, zipped around like a furry helicopter. Wilma the Ladybug, with her red shell and black spots, snoozed peacefully in a crack in the wall. One morning, Bart zoomed over to Wilma, puffing out his tiny chest like a miniature balloon. "Wilma! Did you know I'm practically a superhero of the bug world? I've seen, like, EVERYTHING!" Wilma, peeking out from her crack-bedroom, raised an eyebrow. "Really, Bart? Like what?" "Everything!" Bart declared, his voice booming. "I've traveled the world, you know. I've flown over vast oceans and endless seas. Why, just last week, I was soaring above the mighty Atlantic!"

In reality, Bart's biggest adventure was zooming across the garden's frozen puddle, but hey, who needed facts when you had imagination, right? Wilma, a ladybug who knew a fib when she heard one, just smiled. "Wow, that's amazing, Bart. Tell me more!" Bart, loving the attention, launched into a story about a flower garden so grand and spectacular, it had flowers that glittered like diamonds. It was actually Mr. Thompson's prize-winning rose bushes, but who was keeping track? He even told a whopper about outrunning a giant, feathery monster! Okay, maybe it was a startled sparrow, but close enough!

Wilma listened patiently (winter months were boring anyway), a tiny ladybug giggle escaping every now and then. "You must be braver than a mighty ant army, Bart," she said. "Braver, stronger, wiser – you name it, I've got it!" Bart kept on bragging. "Did you know the stars are these enormous fireflies living in space? And guess what the moon is made of? The creamiest white chocolate you've ever tasted!" Wilma burst out laughing. "Chocolate? That's a new one!"

Suddenly, a gust of wind stronger than Mr. Thompson's leaf blower, slammed the greenhouse door open. Bart, caught by surprise, went flying! He tumbled through the air like a leaf in a whirlwind. With a last desperate flap, he squeezed into a tiny hole in Wilma's wall. Safe at last, but still shivering from his adventure, Bart realized maybe real stories were cooler than made-up ones. After all, who needs to be a superhero when you can survive a winter windstorm? Curled up in his cozy wall nook and overhearing Wilma's giggles, Bart vowed to be a little more honest and a little less braggy from that day on.

Be honest and genuine; you don't need to exaggerate to impress others.

A New Mole Home

Nate the Mole Rat and his wife, Netty, lived underground. Their burrow was comfortable but lately, their fridge (well, the dirt pile they kept snacks in) was looking a little bare. "Time to move!" squeaked Netty, her nose twitching for juicier worms. One chilly February morning, they packed their mole-sized backpacks and headed for the river. The river was like a big, half-frozen ice cube. Scary, but they had to cross to reach tastier dirt. Nate, being a brave mole, found a narrow spot where the ice was thick enough. They inched across, claws digging in for dear life, Netty holding onto Nate's tail. Finally, on the other side!

Under a giant oak tree, they found the perfect spot, soft dirt waiting to be made into a home. Claws flying, they dug a brand-new home with rooms for sleeping, storing snacks, and maybe even a future mole nursery! The new dirt was like a buffet compared to their old place. There were plump earthworms that wiggled like spaghetti, crunchy beetles that tasted like popcorn, and even a leftover stash of yummy roots from last fall. This place was amazing!

A few weeks later, their burrow welcomed five tiny mole babies! Now, finding food was extra important. Every night, Nate ventured out, his nose leading him to the best worm holes. But one night, things went terribly wrong. Nate, looking for a late-night snack, bumped into Tobby the Toad (who everyone knew was a bit greedy). "Hey! Watch where you're digging!" Tobby croaked, puffing out his bumpy belly. "Just looking for dinner," Nate mumbled. "Get out of here!" Tobby continued. Nate couldn't take it anymore and... took a bite out of Tobby's back (not the best idea)! "Ugh, what is this?!" he sputtered, his mouth tingling. "You taste horrible!" "That's called toad poison, silly mole!" Tobby croaked, his voice dripping with sarcasm. Nate, feeling like his mouth was full of spicy peppers, started spitting like crazy.

Just then, a bat swooped down, a juicy worm dangling from its mouth. Nate, desperate for a normal-flavored snack, leaped to catch it. Big mistake number two! An owl, faster than a speeding pizza delivery, snatched the bat right before Nate's nose. The owl, not happy about being interrupted, swiped at Nate with its sharp talons, leaving a nasty scratch on his back.

Hurting and grumpy, Nate finally made it back to Netty. "This place isn't safe!" he groaned, showing off his battle wounds. Netty, after hearing about the toad tantrum, the bat-burger blunder, and the owl attack, knew they had to move again. "Don't worry, Nate," she said, giving him a nuzzle. "We'll find a new home, a safe one, with plenty of worms and no greedy toads. Now, let's get these babies some mud-milk cookies!" The next day, with their little mole babies snuggled in their backpacks, Nate and Netty set off again, on a quest for the perfect, safest, and most importantly, toad-free burrow!

Reacting with anger can lead to bigger problems; it's better to stay calm and talk things through.

The Clothes' Revenge

Kayla's room was a disaster zone! Clothes and toys lived in a messy pile that looked like a washing machine exploded in there. Her favorite Pink-Sweater, had a hole in the elbow and grumbled to Old-Jeans, "Look at this! I keep getting thrown on the floor, and Kayla never fixes me!" Old-Jeans sighed. "At least you're here. My best friend, Left-Sneaker, vanished days ago! Last I heard, he was shoved into a drawer with no escape!" Stuck under the bed, he couldn't even peek over the mountain of clothes.

From behind a chair, a Pair-of-Dirty-Socks, chimed in. "We should be getting a bubble bath in the laundry basket, not a dust bath behind the chair! How will we ever get clean?" Even Party-Dress, crumpled in the corner, felt neglected. "I used to be the star of the show, all sparkly and twirly. Now I'm a forgotten princess, lost in the clothes jungle!"

One morning, Kayla was super excited. It was her friend's birthday party, and she wanted to wear Party-Dress! But uh oh! As Kayla dug through the clothes mountain, Pink-Sweater hid under the bed, Old-Jeans got buried deeper by a runaway toy truck, and Party-Dress... well, Party-Dress became a master of hide-and-seek behind the closet door. The Pair-of-Dirty-Socks? They tangled themselves with the curtains like ninjas, making them impossible to find. "Where did everything go?!" Kayla cried, flinging clothes around in frustration.

The room became even messier! Exhausted and close to tears, Kayla plopped on her bed. Suddenly, she remembered something her mom always said: "A clean room is a happy room!" Maybe it was true? With determination in her eyes, Kayla decided to give it a shot. First, she sorted the clothes into piles. Pair-of-Dirty-Socks got a one-way ticket to the laundry basket. Old-Jeans was rescued from the toy avalanche, and a happy reunion with Left-Sneaker took place! Pink-Sweater was gently pulled out from under the bed, and Kayla promised to ask her mom to fix the hole (no more monster elbows)!

Finally, Party-Dress was freed from her hiding spot, her wrinkles smoothed out with love. As Kayla hung up her clothes and put away her toys, her room transformed from a messy jungle into a neat and tidy space. It felt... well, amazing! And guess what? The clothes seemed happy too! Pink-Sweater wasn't hiding anymore, Old-Jeans and Left-Sneaker were back together, Party-Dress sparkled once again, and even the socks (fresh and clean now) looked happy wiggling their toes in the drawer. Kayla beamed. Finding things was a breeze now! From that day on, Kayla kept her room clean, and her clothes lived happily ever after – in a neat and organized closet, of course!

Keeping things tidy makes life easier and happier for everyone.

The Golden Rain

Once upon a time, in a town so small the mailman knew everyone's dog by name, lived the happiest bunch of folks you could ever meet. They weren't rich in fancy cars or mountains of gold, but they had something way cooler – hearts overflowing with kindness! They helped each other bake cookies, fixed each other's wobbly bikes, and celebrated everything together – from catching the biggest fish, to Mrs. Parker's prize-winning pickles.

Then, one wacky Wednesday, the sky went cuckoo! Instead of raindrops, golden coins started plunking down like some giant piggy bank just exploded! Truth was that a leprechaun was having a terrible day. He tripped over a toadstool, stubbing his toe and sending his pot of gold clattering through the sky, thus raining golden coins.

At first, everyone cheered – free money for everyone! But then, things got a little... well, crazy. Mr. Jones, usually the friendliest fellow, tripped over his own shoelace trying to grab more coins than Mrs. Smith. Kids who used to share toys, started wrestling over shiny coins. The town square, once a place for picnics and laughter, became a coin-collecting battlefield!

Little Austin, with his bright blue eyes and a gap-toothed grin, watched in confusion. He had collected a pile of coins himself, but seeing everyone fight, made his tummy feel weird. He remembered how much fun they had before the golden rain, working together and sharing everything. So, Austin hatched a plan! He grabbed his pile of coins and skipped from house to house, offering some to each family. "Hey, take these," he would say, his voice small but brave. "Remember how we used to be nice? Let's stop fighting and be friends again!"

At first, everyone stared, surprised by Austin's kindness. But as he kept giving away his gold, something magical happened. The greedy frowns melted away, replaced by smiles and shy thank yous. Maybe they had gotten a little carried away by the shiny stuff. Inspired by Austin, others started sharing their coins too.

The grumpy turned friendly, the grabby turned generous, and soon, the town square was filled with laughter and sharing, not fighting. The golden rain may have caused a commotion, but Austin, the bravest little guy in town, reminded everyone that real treasure isn't found in how much gold you have, but in the kindness, you share with your friends. From that day on, the town never forgot Austin's lesson. They used their gold to build a big slide (the best in the whole state), a super-interesting library, and even a swimming pool! And whenever a celebration came around, they didn't just eat cake, they remembered the day the sky rained gold!

True wealth is found in kindness and generosity, not in material riches.

A Threaded Tale

Two best buds lived in a cozy sewing basket, Ned the Needle and Ted the Thread. They were the ultimate stitching team! Zippety-zap, they would mend ripped seams and stitch together the most dazzling dresses. Everyone knew them – the perfect pair in the whole sewing kit! One day, a sassy green button named Gaby, rolled closer to Ned. "Feeling a little stuck with Ted there, aren't you?" she whispered with a sly grin. "He just trails behind, all boring and slow. Why not ditch him and be a free needle?"

Ned, who loved a bit of adventure, tilted his pointy head. Maybe Gaby was right? A life without Ted, going wherever he wanted, sounded pretty sweet! So, the next morning, while the seamstress sewed a sparkly skirt, Ned took a daring leap! He pretended to slip from her fingers and plopped down a dark crack in the floorboards. "Ned! Come back!" Ted cried, his cottony voice echoing. But Ned, picturing a life of freedom, pretended not to hear.

Down in the dusty crack, however, freedom wasn't so fun. Ned couldn't sew anything alone! He poked at cobwebs and tried to stitch dust bunnies, but it was pointless. His pointy tip grew lonely, and his one eye felt tired from all the darkness. Days turned into weeks, and Ned finally realized what a big mistake he had made. He missed Ted! He missed sewing socks and fixing ripped teddy bear tummies. Feeling quite depressed, Ned wished with all his pointy might for the seamstress to find him.

And then, one sunny day, a bright light shone through the crack! The seamstress, with a gasp, spotted Ned's shiny tip. She carefully pulled him out, dusted him off, and – whoosh! – threaded Ted back through his eye. Reunited at last, Ned and Ted sewed with more joy than ever before! They both knew that being a team was what made them special. Ned was lost without Ted's wiggly body, and Ted just flopped around uselessly without Ned's sharp point.

A few days later, while mending a captain's hat, they saw Gaby the button again. She tried whispering her jealous words, but Ned just rolled his eye (if needles could roll eyes). He wasn't falling for that trick again. He had Ted by his side, and together, they could mend anything, even a broken friendship (although Gaby the button might need a whole lot of attitude-mending herself). From that day on, Ned and Ted stuck close together, a perfect pair reminding everyone that true friendship is stronger than any envious whispers, and that teamwork always makes the sewing dream work!

Listening to envious or mean advice can lead to bad choices; avoid letting negative people influence you.

The Hatching Bill

Declan the farmer was a jolly fellow with a wide smile. He traveled from village to village, his cart overflowing with fresh fruits and vegetables. One afternoon, Declan's stomach started singing an empty-tummy tune, after a busy market day. He trotted to the village tavern, ready for a champion-sized lunch. Declan ordered the biggest plate of eggs (four of them) and a bowl of corn that could feed a whole family. He gobbled it all up with a happy sigh, feeling like a king. But as he reached for his pockets to pay the bill, he noticed outside the window two shadowy figures hitching his horse to their cart and taking off in a flash!

"Hey!" Declan yelled, jumping out of his chair as fast as he could. He chased after the thieves with all his might and when he finally got them, he rode his horse towards his village, forgetting all about the unpaid bill. Back at the tavern, Alan the owner, a man with a huge mustache, watched sadly as Declan disappeared in a cloud of dust. He waited and waited for Declan to return, but days turned into weeks, and weeks turned into... a very long time.

A whole year later, Declan came back to the same village, his cart overflowing with juicy apples and plump pumpkins. He sold everything and his pockets were jingling with coins. Feeling hungry and tired, he once again marched back to Alan's tavern for another champion-sized lunch. However, when the bill arrived, Declan's eyes nearly popped out. It cost more than he had earned all day! "Whoa hold on!" he exclaimed, "This looks like a bill for the whole village!" Alan, still a tad angry about last year's unpaid lunch, puffed out his chest and said, "Well, you see, last year, you forgot to pay for your four eggs. If I had used those eggs to hatch some chicks, I would have hundreds of eggs by now! And that corn you ate? I could have planted it and grown a whole cornfield!"

Declan scratched his head, completely confused. This sounded fishier than a day-old fish! He decided to take the tavern owner to court. In court, the wise judge, first listened to Alan's story, while they were waiting for the farmer to arrive.

Then, when Declan finally got there, she turned to him and asked, "Why were you late for court, farmer?" Declan, with a cheeky grin, replied, "Your Honor, I was busy helping a friend boil his seeds for planting!" The courtroom erupted in laughter (even the judge chuckled a bit). Everyone knew boiled seeds wouldn't grow! Declan had a point – just like boiled eggs wouldn't hatch chicks and cooked corn couldn't grow a field. The judge, seeing the logic clear as day, ruled in Declan's favor. Alan grumbled a bit, but fairness is fairness, and he had to accept it. Declan, relieved and happy, paid Alan the real price for his lunch from last year, and they even became friends!

Be fair and reasonable when asking for something; everything will work out in the end.

Walking Wonders

Dylan flung open the curtains – sunshine attacked his eyelids like a swarm of happy bees! It was a perfect Tuesday, and a super idea buzzed in his head. He threw on clothes fast, grabbed his backpack, and rocketed into the kitchen. "Mom!" Dylan yelled, "Can we ditch the bus today and become... walking wonders?" His mom blinked, spilling some coffee. "Walking Wonders? Sounds... interesting. Sure, honey!" With an apple clutched in his hand, Dylan ran out the door.

At the corner, he spotted his best friends, Danny and Mike, waiting like lumps on a log. "Hey dudes!" Dylan said, all excited. "Today, we're not riding the rumble bus – we're WALKING!" Danny scratched his head. "Walking? Why?" "It's, like, exercise for our muscles and good for the planet!" Dylan explained, puffing out his chest (though his muscles weren't exactly wonders yet). "We will save the Earth!" Mike's eyes lit up. "Saving the Earth? Like superheroes, but with legs? I'm in!"

And so, the Walking Wonders began their quest! They walked past houses and speeding cars. They noticed a frozen pond where they could come after school for skating. They saw the bare tree branches reaching towards the winter sky, with a few remaining birds chirping. People were shoveling snow from their driveways. They even high-fived Mr. Jacobs, the old man who lived on Carob Street (he wasn't so moody after all)! "This is way cooler than the bus!" Danny exclaimed. "Who knew our neighborhood could be so interesting?"

Suddenly, a park with swings appeared! The Walking Wonders, with superhero reflexes, took a quick pitstop for some swinging and giggling. Refueled by laughter, they continued their walk, feeling like they could conquer anything – even math class! At school, they were surprised to see their teacher, Mrs. Thomas, with a big smile. "Good morning, Walking Wonders! Woah is that capes I see?" she said, laughing.

Dylan smiled. "We're saving the planet, Mrs. Thomas, one step at a time!" From that day on, Dylan, Danny, and Mike became walking, talking advertisements for leg power. They convinced more and more friends to join their eco-friendly crew. Soon, the whole neighborhood was buzzing with kids walking, biking, and scooting to school. It was like a mini parade of happy faces and fresh air! One day, Dylan's mom asked, "So, how's the Walking Club going?" Dylan winked. "We're not just walking, Mom, we're Walking Wonders!"

Walking, biking, or scootering to school keeps you healthy and helps the environment.

A New Home for Rayna

Rayna was not an average ray of sunshine. She most certainly loved painting rainbows on puddles and tickling sleepy flowers awake, but unlike her sisters who zoomed back to the sun each night, Rayna yearned for more. "The world is a huge playground, Papa Sun!" she would chirp, bouncing with sunshine-y excitement. One day, Papa Sun, a huge ball of fire, told her: "Off you go then, little explorer! But remember, the world is big, and bedtime is important!"

Rayna rocketed towards Earth, a giggling streak of light. She danced on ocean waves, turning them into shimmering fun for dolphins. She tickled the noses of fluffy clouds, making them erupt in giggles of rain. In the jungle, she became friends with the playful monkeys, swinging through the trees and leaving trails of sunshine behind. Days turned into weeks, and Rayna kept exploring. She dipped her toes into the scorching desert sands. Cacti with arms like prickly pears stood tall, their flowers blooming in vibrant reds and purples despite the heat. She chased tumbleweeds that rolled by, giggling as they bounced in the dry wind.

Rayna zoomed through towering buildings made of glass and steel. They were like giants wearing mirrored sunglasses, reflecting the world in a thousand shimmering pieces. Below, cars buzzed like colorful beetles, and people scurried around like busy ants, their chatting rising in a happy hum. Rayna waltzed among meadows overflowing with wildflowers. Poppies swayed like red skirts in a gentle breeze, and daisies peeked up with curious yellow eyes.

Butterflies with wings painted in rainbows flitted past, and bumblebees, fat and fuzzy, whispered secrets to the flowers in their buzzy language. Rayna even spotted a family of playful rabbits, their noses twitching and ears perked, listening to the meadow's stories. But slowly, a strange tiredness crept in. She tried napping under leaves, but they kept rustling. Houses were too stuffy, the mountains too cold, and the ocean too restless.

Rayna, the once energetic ray, felt so tired. Then, while peeking into a fragrant orange grove, she spotted a sight that made her gasp. It was an orange tree, its fruit glowing a warm, inviting orange. As Rayna snuggled inside one, a feeling of pure bliss washed over her. The sweet scent and the juicy embrace were perfect! From then on, Rayna made her home in the sunny oranges. Next time you bite into a juicy orange, remember Rayna, the sunshine adventurer who found her perfect home, in the warm, happy glow of an orange!

It's important to find what works best for you and follow your own path, even if it's unconventional.

FROM THE AUTHOR

I really hope you enjoyed this book. Please consider leaving a review on Amazon.
Just scan the QR code below:

Collect the entire series:
A Year Full of Storytelling

There are four volumes in the "366 Days of Short Tales" series – one for each
season of the year. If you and your little ones enjoyed reading these stories, why
stop? For more delightful and thought-provoking short stories check out the QR
code below...

Made in the USA
Las Vegas, NV
14 December 2024

14337961R00057